PRAISE FOR JAMES MELVILLE AND
A HAIKU FOR HANAE

"Melville's Otani novels could be described by the Japanese adjective *shibui* ... elegant, restrained and in the best possible taste."

Los Angeles Times

"Highly recommended for mystery readers of refined taste."

Chicago Sun-Times

"Fascinating layers of Japanese customs and manners unpeeled as Otani investigates politely. Superior mix of crime and culture."

The London *Times*

"Otani is one of the most expertly drawn figures in modern detective fiction who deserves a wider audience, not just because he is authentic but because he and his world are so original."

Punch

Also by James Melville
Published by Fawcett Books:

Superintendent Otani Mysteries

THE WAGES OF ZEN
A SORT OF SAMURAI
THE CHRYSANTHEMUM CHAIN
THE NINTH NETSUKE
DEATH OF A DAIMYO
SAYONARA, SWEET AMARYLIS
THE DEATH CEREMONY
GO GENTLY, GAIJIN
KIMONO FOR A CORPSE
THE RELUCTANT RONIN

Other Fiction

THE IMPERIAL WAY

A HAIKU FOR HANAE

James Melville

FAWCETT CREST • NEW YORK

For Clare and Jamie,
with love

Author's Note

I have tried to describe the island of Awaji and its principal town of Sumoto as they really were when I first visited them over twenty years ago and, to a large extent, still miraculously were in the late 1980s. This is, however, a work of fiction, and the Sumoto of my story is not the real town. The actual Shinto shrine in Sumoto is not of the Inari type, and it bears no resemblance to the one I have invented. There are a number of traditional inns in the town: none of them is the model for the Tokiwa. Above all, the characters in this story are without exception figments of my imagination.

The peculiarly Japanese phenomenon of fox possession has interested a great many researchers, both Japanese and foreign. Lafcadio Hearn—who lived for a time in the ancient province of Izumo—wrote a charming essay ("Kitsune" from the book *Glimpses of Unfamiliar Japan*) about it in the 1890s: it is well worth reading. By far the most authoritative modern survey in English of the whole subject of Japanese shamanistic beliefs and practices is Carmen Blacker's fascinating *The Catalpa Bow* (Allen & Unwin, 2nd ed., 1986).

James Melville

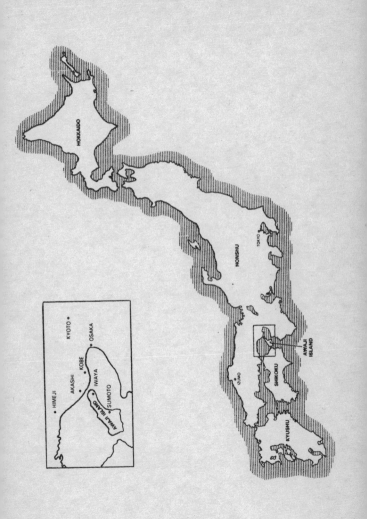

The Japanese version of the title reads
Kitsune-Bi ("Fox-Fire") and the calligraphy is
by Mie Kimata

Prelude:
The Present

HANAE OTANI SMILED AS SHE WATCHED HER HUSBAND screw up his eyes to peer at the illuminated panel above the bank of ticket machines at Sannomiya Station in Kobe and then resignedly take out his glasses and put them on so as to be able to decipher the fare to Akashi. In the taxi from their house in the foothills of suburban Mount Rokko she had thought to ask him if he had enough change, and been slightly surprised when he produced one of the new "orange cards" from his pocket with something of a flourish. It was good for ten thousand yen's worth of travel on newly privatized Japan Railways and had a color photograph of the seafront at Miyazaki on the reverse. That was where they had spent their frugal honeymoon all those years before, and Hanae was still thinking back to those hungry, uncertain, make-do-and-mend days as she drifted away from the muddle of people at the machines and waited for him.

Having reached and inserted his card into the machine, pressed the right buttons and collected their tickets Superintendent Tetsuo Otani of the Hyogo prefectural police force joined Hanae in front of a large advertising poster depicting a gracious, well-upholstered lady of mature years looking appreciatively at her equally well-preserved male escort. The

1

male model wore an immaculate cream-colored suit; the woman a pale blue dress and a white hat with a vast brim. Otani recognized her as a film star of the fifties who still occasionally put in an appearance in television dramas, usually as a dignified senior professional woman such as a doctor or a professor.

"What's the matter, Ha-chan, envious?"

"Envious? What on earth are you talking about?"

Otani half turned and pointed to the poster. "It looked as though you were wishing we were setting off with a special Full Moon one-week travel pass, expensive false teeth and a new set of matching suitcases like that pair. We're certainly eligible, after all. You only have to be eighty-eight between you and we're well over—"

"Don't you dare remind me!"

"Suit yourself," Otani said cheerfully. "Tell you something, though, they're going to spend a fortune on dry-cleaning going round the country got up like that. Come on, the next fast train's in eight minutes."

At around ten-thirty on a Tuesday in May the commuter rush was long over. Nevertheless there were plenty of people on the move, and not only the usual mid-morning mix of students and housewives. The period beginning on April 29 with the Emperor's Birthday and ending with Boys' Day on May 5 is known to all in Japan as Golden Week because May Day is also a public holiday, and many office workers take advantage of the string of three days off by inserting a couple of days' leave in the spaces to make a week of it. That had been the previous week, when Otani had, as was his habit, done exactly the opposite. He had put himself down for duty throughout the holiday period, thereby earning the grateful thanks of Inspector Jiro Kimura, who wanted to go on a package tour to Europe to brush up his French and buy himself some new clothes in Italy.

Kimura was one of the three senior headquarters inspectors on whom Otani most depended, and his first choice to stand in for him in his absence. The scholarly Takeshi Hara was too young and too much of a newcomer to be in the running, and the veteran "Ninja" Noguchi, though by far the most senior of the three in age and experience, was the first to agree that he wasn't much of a hand at paperwork. More than once he had added that in any case except in dire emergency it was too much of an effort to try to make himself presentable enough for any job involving dealings with senior officials of the prefectural government.

By the end of Golden Week, therefore, Otani had enjoyed a tranquil interlude clearing up odds and ends of work at his desk, Kimura had returned in an elegant silk suit by Giorgio Armani rejoicing in the strength of the Japanese yen, and now the Otanis were off to spend a few days on Awaji island, which lies like a misshapen pear in the Inland Sea a few miles west of Kobe.

They found seats on the left-hand side of the train and Hanae gazed contentedly out at the seemingly endless western suburbs of Kobe while Otani glanced through the newspaper. By the time they reached Suma fifteen minutes later he had finished with it and was ready for more conversation.

"When did you last come this way?"

"I really can't remember. Not for a good many years. In fact, not since that awful business at Himeji Castle, I think. And that was, what, nearly eight years ago."

Otani grunted, and shuddered involuntarily as Hanae's words brought vividly to his mind's eye the look on the crazed gardener's face as they had grappled in the moonlight at the top of the mighty stone ramparts and then toppled over the two-foot hedge. He would never forget that fall into the black waters of the moat thirty feet below, the murderer clutching at him in a grotesque parody of an embrace; or the terror of the following few minutes until he was dragged out barely conscious, chilled, vomiting and filthy with slime.

"I'm sorry," Hanae said, looking at him with concern. "It was silly of me to mention it."

Otani pulled himself together. "It could have been worse. But I can well imagine you hardly paid attention to the scenery on the way to see me in hospital." He gestured toward the window. "Look at all those new hotels and seaside apartments."

Between Suma and Akashi the railway follows the coastline, often no more than two hundred yards from the sea, which was as blue and sparkling as a picture in a travel agency brochure in the sunshine that day. The huddle of drab-looking little houses pressing close to the line further east had in this stretch given way to altogether more spacious developments. Jaunty striped awnings adorned the windows of apartment blocks provided with that wonder of wonders in Japan, adequate car parks. Hotels and restaurants had sprung up, many of them with terraces to the seaward side bright with outside tables shaded by multicolored umbrellas, and often enough provided with cunningly placed palm trees to emphasize the Riviera look.

"My goodness, it *has* changed, hasn't it?"

Otani's smile was slightly twisted. "It certainly has. Of course, a lot of people live in those flats all the time and commute to work in Kobe or even Osaka, but you'd be surprised how many are just weekend and holiday places, empty most of the time."

"What sort of people can afford to be so extravagant?"

"These days, all sorts. The divisional inspector from Akashi's been reporting a rash of the sort of crime you might expect when people have money to burn and time on their hands."

Hanae would have liked him to go into a little more detail but Otani fell silent and said nothing more until the train stopped at Akashi and they got out. They were traveling light, and ignoring the line of taxis outside the station Otani set off at a great pace with their two modest bags through a dense thicket of parked bicycles. Hanae picked her way through more delicately and caught up with him outside a branch of the Mitsubishi Bank on a corner at the other side of a busy main road. He gestured expansively.

"It's only a few minutes down this way to the ferry. Look, there's a signpost pointing to it." Hanae was glad to see that he seemed to have pushed the recollection of the Himeji affair back where it belonged and to have recovered his normal composure. Turning left, they set off again together at a more leisurely pace down a road lined with restaurants, small boutiques, travel agencies and sporting-goods shops. It was

4

no more than a few hundred yards to the harbor and the Awaji island ferry terminal, where Otani established that they had twenty-five minutes to wait, bought their tickets and then looked round the shabby old waiting room with satisfaction.

"Well, thank goodness *this* is still the same. The fare's gone up of course, but it looks just like it did twenty years ago, apart from all these fancy launches in the harbor along with the fishing boats."

Hanae pointed to a huge banner stretched out on a nearby wall. Painted on it in characters two feet high was the slogan LET'S COMPLETE THE GREAT AKASHI BRIDGE IN A HURRY!

"Not quite, I'm afraid," she said. "It won't be long before there'll be no need for the ferry, and Awaji won't be a proper island anymore. Sad. But then of course that's why Akira and Akiko came here, isn't it?"

"Yes. Akira's no sentimentalist, even if he has thrown up a good safe job. If you're going to go into the market-gardening business it makes sense to be a jump ahead of the competition. That land they bought last year has already doubled in value as other people have realized what a difference it's going to make to marketing when the road's built. He'll be able to load up that pick-up van of theirs and drive straight to central Kobe in about forty-five minutes."

Hanae looked at her husband sideways in silence. She knew how much he hated most of what passed for progress in modern Japan, and was touched by his brave attempt to find an argument in favor of the monstrous bridges which were turning his beloved Inland Sea into a complex of motorways. Then he smiled.

"Yes, and of course it'll be much easier for Akiko to bring Kazuo to see us. There's bound to be bus services, and now that he's getting to be such a big boy maybe they'll even let him come on his own and stay with us for a few days now and then."

"I doubt that. The poor lad would be bored to tears without his friends and his toys. Come on, let's get on the boat."

Hanae stayed out of the breeze when the battered old ferry got under way a few minutes later, but Otani spent most of the twenty-five-minute trip by the rail in the sunshine. She joined him during the last few minutes, when the boat was edging into the little harbor at Iwaya. "Some nice old houses still," he said. "But that big national hospital wasn't here when I had that murder case to look into. Hard to believe it was about twenty years ago. I've been thinking about that business."

"So have I. Remember the beautiful *haiku* you wrote for me?"

His throat suddenly constricted, Tetsuo Otani looked into his wife's eyes and saw that she was smiling through tears. Of course he remembered, and it was too much to hope that she might have forgotten even after so many years.

Chapter 1
February 1968

"IT REALLY *IS* A MISERABLE SORT OF DAY . . . BUT THEN what can you expect in February, even in Awaji?" The words were conventional, and the pale moon face that made Inspector Saburo Takada look too young to be within a few months of retirement was expressionless. Only his voice betrayed his age, but his tone suggested utter despair rather than a philosophical acceptance of the facts of life on the part of the speaker.

The inspector occupied a small but by no means uncomfortable office on the floor above what passed for the main action at the Sumoto divisional headquarters. He and Otani were sipping green tea, and Takada kept looking out of the window. A gentle but persistent drizzle had produced dark patches here and there on the windward side of the mostly wooden buildings across the street, like sweat-stains on the shirt of a man exerting himself on a hot day.

It was just after three forty-five. Otani had arrived at the ferry terminal at Iwaya an hour or so earlier, and had been at the police headquarters in Sumoto for about fifteen minutes. He was disappointed that Inspector Takada had reverted to the subject of the weather. This had already been exhaustively discussed, after Takada had met him at the ferry and assured his colleague from prefectural headquarters in Kobe that he and every officer serving under him in Awaji was honored by his presence on the island.

Being nearly twenty years younger than Takada as well as very much his junior in the rank they both held, Otani had responded as convention demanded by expressing delighted astonishment that the inspector had gone in person all the way to Iwaya to greet him, and apologized profusely for disturbing him at what was no doubt a particularly busy time. On the way to the waiting car it had been Takada's turn again. It was hardly raining at all at Iwaya, but he opened the spare umbrella he had brought along for Otani and urged him to use it during their ten-yard walk, regretting elaborately that he could not have had the pleasure of welcoming his visitor on a more pleasant day.

The conversational preliminaries unavoidable in Japan once out of the way, Otani had rather expected to get on to the subject of murder during the twenty-mile drive down the east-coast road to Sumoto. Instead Takada drew his attention to the wayward shrines, tiny shops or other unremarkable sights they passed every few hundred yards, announced at the appropriate moment the name of each of the dozen fishing villages between Iwaya and Sumoto, and at odd moments in between lectured him like a tour guide.

On their arrival it was of course only to be expected that Takada would apologize yet again, this time for the shabbiness and general inadequacy of the premises and the untidiness of his own office, which Otani quite liked. A tourist office calendar featuring a photograph of the famous whirlpools at Naruto hung on the wall to the left of a desk innocent of paperwork. On the one behind Otani was a large poster illustrating the varieties of official traffic signs both mandatory and advisory, and an eye-test chart with rows of phonetic Japanese characters in descending order of size. Otani had noticed it as he sat down, surreptitiously closing his right eye and trying and failing to make out the bottom line with the left. He hadn't seen a chart like it for several years. The optician at the shop where he had recently bought a pair of

8

reading glasses used an ingenious illuminated box and a contrivance that made Otani see green and red circles.

"Ah, well, it's noticeably milder here than in Kobe, and we have spring to look forward to before long," Otani said briskly, having decided that enough was enough. He pressed on before Takada could embark on any more banalities. "Well now, according to our records this is the first case of murder in Awaji for many years."

Takada looked as though he was near to tears, and the muscles round his mouth worked for several seconds as he forced himself to refer at last to the distasteful reason for Otani's presence in his office. "That such a thing should have happened to us!" he almost wailed. "And a foreigner of all people! A hundred thousand Japanese live contentedly on Awaji, Inspector, and we welcome thousands of tourists from other parts of Japan every year. People here try, I'm sure, to do their best for the very occasional foreign sightseer, though there are really no suitable hotels and of course they can't eat our food or use chopsticks—"

"But this young American wasn't a tourist, was he?" Otani's own view of Westerners was hardly more sympathetic than Inspector Takada's, but it was obvious to him that he had to be ruthless in cutting short a monologue about their unattractive eccentricities.

"That's what I mean, you see. It's bad enough when they come sightseeing, and infinitely worse to have a pair of them *living* here. They were bound to give trouble."

"A case of murder is certainly troublesome, but most of all to the victim, I should have thought."

Takada looked first puzzled and then deeply suspicious. Otani inferred that he belonged to the influential school of police thought which held that the great majority of people who got themselves killed other than accidentally were almost certainly intolerable nuisances who had been asking for it. This theory was plausible enough given that most murders which came to the attention of the police in Japan were committed either by a member of the victim's family or in the course of disputes among gangsters over spheres of influence.

9

"Be that as it may," Takada went on with a touch of hauteur, "in such highly unusual circumstances involving a *gaijin* I thought it proper to leave the investigation entirely to the experts."

Otani was astounded to hear this. "You mean that no inquiries whatever have been made since the body was discovered yesterday morning?"

"None. I judged it wise to leave you a clear field for your own inquiries."

A wild thought struggled to the surface in Otani's mind, and he cleared his throat noisily before expressing it. "The, er, the body isn't still lying there, by any chance?"

Takada seemed to have got over his momentary irritation with Otani. He settled back in his chair and sighed as he shook his head slowly. "I regret not. I suppose that would have been the best course really, wouldn't it, but apparently the doctor who examined the body initially insisted that it should be taken to the mortuary." Then he brightened. "It was photographed *in situ*, though. I distinctly remember being told that. You know, when I was young we always used to worry about whether or not snaps would *come out*, but I understand they always do nowadays. So I expect ours have. I must get someone to show them to you."

On the way from Kobe Otani had reminded himself repeatedly to be mindful of the sensitivities of the local officer in charge who might well resent having to cooperate with a much younger man from headquarters. Now he gazed at Inspector Takada in a state of mind approaching awe. He knew that the Awaji division had no criminal investigation section as such. It was therefore right and proper for Takada to have called him in. On the other hand Otani could hardly credit the man's apparently total lack of interest in what must surely be the most newsworthy crime ever committed during his command of the Awaji division.

"Yes. I see. A clear field. Thank you. I take it you didn't visit the scene of the crime yourself, then?"

"No. Most of yesterday I was at the city hall. Closeted, you know, with the mayor and the head of the financial affairs department going through the municipal budget for the com-

10

ing financial year. You'll appreciate that it's a considerable privilege for me to be invited to be a party to their discussions. In the circumstances it would have been the height of discourtesy to have made some specious excuse and left them stranded.''

"I see. So your deputy presumably took charge on the spot.''

"Unfortunately, Assistant Inspector Kuroda is away at present on some course or other at the prefectural training center. I'm afraid I can't recall precisely what it is about. One of these management topics so fashionable nowadays, no doubt. No, young Higashida bustled about and did everything necessary. So I thought the best thing would be to offer you his services while you clear everything up. Would that be satisfactory, I wonder? After all, you won't want me getting under your feet, and I do have rather a lot to occupy me at present . . . I shall, naturally, be most interested to know in due course who killed the American. With a bit of luck the other one will probably go away now, wouldn't you think?''

One of Otani's great assets as a police detective was his poker face, but in such an unusual situation it was all he could do to maintain it. He chose his words with care. "Thank you. This conversation has been most helpful, but I do realize I've already taken up far too much of your own time. I very much appreciate your giving me such a free hand, and the offer of Assistant Inspector Higashida's help . . .'' He paused in the face of Takada's seraphic smile and half-suppressed chuckle.

"Oh dear, you're rather premature, I'm afraid. One of these fine days, perhaps, but Higashida's a patrolman, not an assistant inspector. Bright, though. I must in all fairness grant him that. I'll get him up here and you can form your own opinion of him. I know, I'll ask him to bring whatever he has in the way of papers, too. I'm sure you'll be interested.''

"I've reserved you a room at the Tokiwa Inn, sir. It's only five minutes' walk from here, but if you'd prefer to go by car . . . ?''

"No, let's walk. I don't have much in the way of luggage, as you see." Otani was wearing a raincoat over an unobtrusive blue suit, and had brought with him two pairs of socks, two shirts and two changes of underwear wrapped in a large russet-colored silk square. Apart from the clean clothes the bundle contained his old-fashioned open razor, two packets of Peace Brand cigarettes and a recent Japanese translation of Agatha Christie's *Cat Among the Pigeons* Hanae had bought for him and slipped in as a surprise present, knowing that he was amused by Hercule Poirot through really more of a Nero Wolfe fan. As the turn of the decade approached more and more Japanese were taking to carrying briefcases, zip-up bags and even suitcases with them on their travels, but Otani knew of nothing so flexible and convenient as a silk *furoshiki* which when not in use could be folded up and slipped into a jacket pocket.

Otani now had under his arm the cardboard envelope file handed over to him in Takada's office but as yet unopened, and Patrolman Higashida seized the modest silk-wrapped bundle as they set off down the street. One CID inspector and patrolman who looked about twenty-five or so constituted a modest enough investigative resource, Otani thought, but he was already in a better mood than he had been when Inspector Takada ushered them both out of his presence with evident relief after the briefest of introductions, muttering that he looked forward to a round-up conference when what he referred to as "this unfortunate distraction" had been satisfactorily dealt with.

Higashida was tidily and compactly built, and just a shade taller than Otani, who reflected that he must have been a wartime baby. He was having to get used to being towered over by the newest recruits to the force, but it was comforting to have a temporary assistant he could look straight in the eye. Higashida's eyes were full of lively intelligence and Otani supposed he was good-looking, in spite of the remains of a few pimples around the chin area and the savagely cropped hair that made his scalp look like a well-used shoe-brush but was now decently covered by his cap.

"It'll be convenient to be within walking distance of headquarters. Fair-sized place, is it, the Tokiwa?'' he asked as they turned a corner into a narrow street, hardly more than an alley.

''Not all that big, sir, but good class. About half a dozen rooms, I should think, maybe ten. They're only ever full in the season, but it's a select sort of restaurant too, by arrangement. The mayor sometimes entertains important visitors there. You should be comfortable enough, but that wasn't the only reason for choosing it.''

''Oh?''

Higashida slackened his pace. ''Sir, I hope you won't think me presumptuous . . .'' he began, and then hesitated. Otani stopped in his tracks and turned to face him.

''Officer Higashida, it would appear that you are the person at Sumoto divisional headquarters who knows most about this case. You have also been assigned to assist me, and I'm sure you'll do that most effectively. So let me make it clear at the outset that I count on your fullest cooperation. You mustn't hesitate to tell me anything you think might be remotely relevant. Now then, why are you putting me in the Tokiwa?''

The young rank-and-file policeman and the seasoned senior officer stared at each other for a long moment, after which Otani knew that they were going to get on with each other.

''Yes, sir. I'll do my best. Well, to begin with it's one of only three or four suitable places in town for an official like you to stay, so nobody will see anything out of the ordinary about it. Secondly, it's not only convenient for headquarters, it's also quite close to the Inari Shrine where the body was found.''

''And thirdly?'' Otani could see there was something else to come.

''Thirdly, sir, I have a strong suspicion that the people at the inn might know something about this affair.''

Chapter 2

Intrigued by what Higashida had said, Otani was tempted to quiz him at length before checking in at the Tokiwa Inn. On the other hand he didn't wish to make himself conspicuous by stopping to hold a long conversation with a uniformed policeman in a public place, so he gleaned as much as he could on the way. By the time they arrived at the inn he had learned more than enough to identify the kimono-clad lady who welcomed him as Mrs. Etsuko Suekawa, the wife of the proprietor.

The inn was a two-storey wooden building in the traditional style, with vertical lattices screening the ground-floor windows on the street side. It could easily have been taken for a spacious private house were it not for the discreet sign to one side of the entrance. This consisted of a simple slab of wood with four Chinese characters deeply incised in it and gilded: from top to bottom the first two read *ryokan*, or inn, and the others *tokiwa*, or evergreen.

Either Mrs. Suekawa was psychic or she had been on the lookout for them, because the sliding door stood open and she was already on her knees on the tatami matting of the raised part of the small lobby, bowing low and murmuring courtesies as the two men entered and Higashida announced his superior. It was a few seconds before she raised her head and Otani was able to see her face; a carefully made-up face but one intrinsically well worth looking at anyway. Otani judged Etsuko Suekawa to be in her late thirties, about five years younger than himself. When he had untied his laces and was ready to step up out of his shoes on to the highly polished wooden step she rose to her feet to usher him in. She was tall for a Japanese woman, perhaps five feet four or five. At this point a maid appeared from the inner regions of the inn and with a perfunctory nod of the head seized the raincoat Otani had removed on entering and his bundle of belongings and followed behind, disposing of the raincoat somewhere en route. Patrolman Higashida evidently planned to join the procession but undoing his bootlaces proved to be a protracted business and Otani paused to wait for him.

A row of backless slippers awaited at the beginning of a corridor of polished dark wood and they each stepped into a pair as Mrs. Suekawa led the way along a short ground-floor corridor, pointing out the entrance to the bathroom on their left. The usual sliding door with opaque glass panels was ajar and as he passed it with a casual glance Otani noted with interest that part of a face and one beady eye appeared in the gap, to be withdrawn with equal abruptness when spotted.

The staircase and upstairs corridor were also of lustrous wood, and even before Mrs. Suekawa paused outside the third sliding door on the right and sank to her knees again to open it, Otani had decided that in spite of the disconcerting apparition at the bathroom door the Tokiwa would suit him very well.

Well versed in the rituals of arriving at a traditional Japanese inn, Otani obediently settled himself on a *zabuton* cushion at the lower lacquer table, in the place of honor with his back to the alcove in which hung a scroll painting—of a spray of plum blossom—in the Chinese style. He was quite ready for the cake and green tea which he knew would be fetched shortly. Higashida put Otani's bundle in a corner and made himself quite at home, seating himself at the other side of the table. The maid had already disappeared, and after a further flurry of courtesies Mrs. Suekawa took her leave.

15

"This is a very pleasant room," Otani said, glancing round. "Eight mats, I see. Spacious." In fact it was bigger, because in addition to the roughly twelve-feet-square tatami-matted area in which they were sitting there was a wooden-floored space by the window big enough to accommodate a glass-topped table and two Western-style easy-chairs made of cane. The sliding *shoji* screens were open and the glazed window beyond overlooked a small garden.

"I'm sure they'll make you comfortable, sir."

"Well, Mrs. Suekawa certainly seems anxious to please." He looked at his watch. "Just after four. A bit early for the bath, perhaps, or is it fed by a hot spring?"

"There is a proper resort area just south of Sumoto, but I should think they can tap the spring in town too. I'm not sure what the arrangement is in this place, but they've been expecting you so the bath's bound to be ready for you anyway whenever you like . . ." Higashida broke off as the door rattled open again and the maid appeared with a large tray which she put beside the table. In silence she placed before each of them a small cup without a handle on a lacquered wooden saucer, and a matching lacquered plate. Otani was pleased to see that on each plate was a lump of bean jelly and a bamboo spear to eat it with. He liked bean jelly rather better than Japanese cakes.

"My name is Otani," he said politely to the maid as she poured them each a cup of green tea from a small kettle and then topped it up with hot water from the thermos jug on the tray. "Please show your favor to me."

It was a routine cliché, but the girl's response was barely civil. "Ito, Noriko." She stated her name as though being interviewed in an official context. Otani liked her small, perky-looking face, but her expression as she got up was one of disdain, and he watched her with some curiosity as she left the room. Then he turned back to Higashida, who had gone brick-red.

"You didn't have time to tell me about that young lady. She doesn't seem to approve of me."

"Very sorry, sir."

"I don't see why you should be the one to apologize. She's

16

an attractive girl, don't you think? Or could be, if she allowed herself to smile now and then. Who is she, a daughter, niece or something?''

Higashida still looked acutely embarrassed. He opened his mouth to speak but then closed it again, got up, went over to the door and peeped out. Only when apparently satisfied that there was nobody within earshot did he return to his zabuton and begin to answer Otani's question. ''Miss Ito is an unusual person, sir. Not related to the Suekawas in any way so far as I know. She comes from a farming family near Hiroda, about ten or twelve miles southwest of here. Right in the middle of the island. She . . . ah, seems to have quarreled with her family over some marriage plan they had for her and decided to make her own way. She, well, the fact is, sir, that she's known to the police.''

''Known? You mean she's committed some offense?''

Higashida's face was a study. ''Oh, no. Nothing like that. It's just that she's a communist, you see. Subscribes to their daily paper, the *Red Flag*. And attends party meetings. Quite openly—she's what you might call forthright about her opinions. So, well, sir, you know that what with the plans for the International Exposition in Osaka in 1970, and the things the student radicals are beginning to get up to in Tokyo and Kyoto, we've all been alerted to keep an eye—''

''Yes, yes, of course. I drafted some of those circulars you've seen.'' Otani suddenly realized that Noriko Ito had looked at him in very much the way his teenage daughter Akiko had taken to doing when they got into arguments about the role of the police in modern Japanese society. ''So you very sensibly keep an eye on this dangerous subversive.'' A brief smile illuminated his swarthy face. ''But you don't really think she's a menace to society, do you? In fact, forgive me for being personal, but I get the impression that you like her.''

''She's a very intelligent person, sir. And yes, I do like her.''

Higashida said this a little defiantly, and Otani found his willingness to speak out to a much more senior officer refreshing in a humble patrolman. ''Even on the strength of

17

the briefest of acquaintances, I can see why. Well now, when you mentioned your reasons for choosing this place on the way here, did you mean to include Miss Ito among those who . . . ?"

"She's bound to have theories, sir, she's that sort of person. I can't see her cooperating in a police inquiry, though."

"Probably not. Still . . ." Otani gazed expressionlessly at the young man. "If by any chance you were to run into her off duty and get into purely social conversation with her, it might be worth raising the subject." He sat up straighter and his manner became briskly businesslike. "Good. Well now, Patrolman Higashida. Thank you for your invaluable help this afternoon. I'm sure we shall work well together. Now I think I shall study this file of yours at leisure and maybe have a look round the Inari Shrine in the morning. I can easily find my way to headquarters, so shall we meet there at, say, eleven? Good. Till tomorrow, then. Oh, and by the way, I think it would be preferable for you to wear plain clothes while we're on this case. If Inspector Takada should query it I'll explain when I see him."

Left to himself Otani removed his shirt, tie, jacket, trousers and socks and slipped into the freshly laundered *yukata* he took from a large, deep tray that contained also a neatly folded sash, a small and somewhat threadbare towel and a padded outer kimono. Wonder of wonders, there was a small hanging space in the built-in cupboard where the bedding was kept when not in use, so he was able to put his clothes away out of sight rather than hooking a coathanger to the wooden rail at the top of the brown plaster wall as one usually had to at inns. There was a new and complicated-looking kerosene heater in the room that made it comfortably warm, and he took the file over to the window area and sat in one of the cane chairs to leaf through it.

Inspector Takada's managerial style was clearly nonchalant to the point of serious dereliction of duty, and for him to have allowed a patrolman to assume unsupervised such a burden of responsibility was outrageous. On the other hand Higashida seemed to have risen to the challenge and used his highly irregular freedom of action to impressive effect. The file was well organized, the material in it intelligently assembled, and Higashida's own report succinct and clearly written.

Otani had known before Takada's exasperated outburst, indeed before he left Kobe, that the dead man, Craig Kington, was one of only two non-Japanese residents on the island of Awaji, the other being his partner Gary Wilson. He knew also that the two Americans held valid visas to work as missionaries, a vocation of which he rather disapproved.

Like the vast majority of his fellow countrymen and women Otani was a casual Buddhist in the sense that he expected his funeral to be conducted in due course by a Buddhist priest; with luck one from the temple near his home in which his late father's memorial tablet was preserved. Again, like most of his compatriots he visited Shinto shrines on appropriate occasions. Needless to say, he and Hanae had been married according to Shinto rites. During the first three days of every new year they joined millions of others in making an offering to the Shinto deities, and they had taken their daughter Akiko to the local shrine in the November of the year in which she was three and again when she was seven to pray for her health and future welfare. And very pretty the shy little girl had looked, too, in her colorful traditional finery.

Otani knew about Christianity, of course, and was acquainted with one or two Japanese Christians. He regarded them as harmless eccentrics, had only the vaguest idea of what they believed and no interest whatever in finding out more. It seemed that the dead man had been a particular kind of Christian: a Mormon, whatever that might be. According to the photocopy of his entry in the aliens' register maintained at Sumoto municipal offices Craig Kington was twenty-six at the time of his death, single, and had been born in Salt Lake City, Utah.

Otani was not at all surprised to discover that the Sumoto police had opened their own file on Kington when he turned up with Gary Wilson in late September 1967. Simply as a foreigner he was worthy of note. A careful hand—not Higashida's—had entered the address of his lodgings in Sumoto and the impressions of the local policeman whose job it was to know who lived where and keep an eye open for unconventional behavior on his patch.

Within a couple of weeks of the appearance of the two men the police knew that Kington had graduated from Brigham Young University in his home state and that he spoke Japanese tolerably well, having undergone intensive language training for four months in Tokyo before moving to Awaji. His (and his partner's) invariably neat appearance had been thought worthy of note. They were, it seemed, never seen in public except in unobtrusive dark suits, white shirts and sober ties. So they were not the hairy, scruffy sort who turned up in Japan having previously drifted through Nepal and Thailand in search of enlightenment and cheap drugs, the *furyo gaijin* or "undesirable aliens" the respectable Japanese of the sixties viewed with mingled fascination and distaste.

Otani had noticed the separate plastic envelope in the file which contained a number of photographs, but having reflected at the time that Inspector Takada would be gratified to know that they had "come out" had put off the unpleasant task of studying them. Now he slipped them out and spread them on the glass top of the table, only to gather them up again quickly and turn them over as he heard the voice of Mrs. Suekawa outside his door.

Almost immediately she entered, all decorous smiles, to inform him that the bath was ready for him at any time and that with his permission his evening meal would be served in his room on his return. The question of drink had then to be discussed and resolved. Otani voted for a bottle of beer rather than *sake* to go with his meal, and the matter being settled picked up his little towel, preparing to follow Mrs. Suekawa. Then, noticing the way she was eyeing the open file on the table, he slipped the photographs back into it and tucked it firmly under his arm. It would probably go limp in the steamy atmosphere of the bathroom, but that wouldn't matter nearly so much as leaving it where the personnel of the Tokiwa could have a good look through its contents.

Chapter 3

"**N**O, FROM A PAYPHONE IN THE LOBBY . . . OH, FINE. No, really. A splendid bath and a really first-class meal . . . particularly good crayfish, and you know how I like them . . . What? . . . Well, hardly, I have only been here a few hours, you know . . . yes, I will, I promise . . . No, earlier I was intending to go out for a stroll but it's come on to rain again so it'll have to wait. How about you, all well? . . . Good . . . She said *what*? . . . How extraordinary . . . Well, naturally, I can see you would be. Tell me more . . . I see. Look, Ha-chan, this is a bit of a shock. I shall have to think about it. Tell you what, I'll ring you again tomorrow, probably from the office, it'll be more convenient . . ."

When he finally put the phone down a couple of minutes later Otani was relieved that Hanae had quickly grasped that he couldn't speak as freely as he would have wished, even from the payphone rather than the extension in his room which would have had to be connected through the inn's small switchboard. The news about Akiko was seriously disquieting. It was understandable that as a first-year student at Kobe University she was excited by the daily protest meetings and lively arguments about university reform. The son of a once eminent professor of chemistry at Osaka Univer-

21

sity, Otani knew a thing or two about the authoritarian way universities were run and had a certain sympathy with some of Akiko's complaints. All the same, if she had indeed decided to join one of the extreme Maoist factions of the All-Japan Student Federation she could find herself in very deep water.

"Please forgive my disturbing you, sir."

"What? Oh, I beg your pardon." Otani had been staring unseeingly at the telephone, too lost in thought to notice that he was no longer alone.

"Allow me to introduce myself. My name is Suekawa, proprietor of this establishment. We are honored by such distinguished patronage, though I fear that our poor facilities . . ." Otani let him burble on while sizing up the husband of the disturbingly attractive lady who had brought his meal to his room and chatted to him so pleasantly while he ate. This in itself was not out of the way. Solitary guests are uncommon in Japanese inns, and it is considered only polite to keep them company over the evening meal.

The proprietor was much less prepossessing than his wife. He was one of those skinny, ageless Japanese with too many teeth for his mouth, two of the most visible being false ones made of cheap metal. His hair was thin, brushed straight back from his forehead without a parting, and so uniformly black that Otani was sure it was dyed. He was dressed very casually, in baggy gray trousers and a check shirt open at his scrawny neck, the sleeves rolled high to reveal whipcord muscles.

Listening with only half an ear to what the man was saying Otani nevertheless gathered that he was apologizing for the inedibility of the food, and realized that it was time he said something. "On the contrary, it was delicious. A remarkably good meal. Did I understand you to say that you are yourself the cook?"

"I do my poor best, sir. I was trained in the catering business and first took care of the cooking here while my father was still alive. It's a family concern, sir, and I inherited the place when he died three years ago. I suppose I ought to engage a cook to take my place, but some of our regular

22

patrons have been good enough to insist that I should carry on." He smirked. "They won't hear of my bringing in anybody else."

"Ah, I see. Well, they obviously appreciate good food when they taste it, and I may say I'm already looking forward myself to tomorrow evening. Well, I'll be getting back to my room—"

"If I may detain the inspector just one moment . . . this letter has arrived for you, sir. By hand."

"For me? Oh, thank you." Otani took the proffered envelope, which was addressed to him in fine brushwork by full name and rank, and ostentatiously sealed across the flap not only with the usual abbreviated form of the character meaning "closed" but also with a blob of sealing wax. Suekawa seemed to be on the point of launching into explanations but Otani headed him off by popping the envelope into the folder he had kept firmly tucked under one arm throughout his phone call to Hanae and with a decisive "Goodnight" made for the stairs.

It was still only about eight in the evening, but when he got back to his room he found the maid Noriko just finishing putting down his bed for him. She had stowed the low table on its side in one corner, closed the shoji screens to conceal the little balcony area, and spread the futon on the tatami mats. The overhead light—an incongruous fluorescent tube—made the room coldly bright, and as Otani entered she was bending to plug in a small bedside lamp placed beside the futon, its lead trailing across the floor.

"Ah. Thank you."

"Bit early, sorry." It was early, even by the peculiar standards of Japanese inns in which a nine or nine-thirty bedtime is taken for granted. All the same Otani was not displeased. However perfunctorily, Noriko was apologizing, and this offered him a possible approach to conversation.

"That's quite all right. I expect you've had a long day. High time you went off duty." The fact that she was about to do so was obvious. Earlier, Noriko had been wearing an apron over a plain dark-blue kimono, its sleeves caught back with tapes to keep her arms free: the conventional dress for

23

a maid in a Japanese-style inn. Now she had on jeans and a sloppy sweater which made her little body look both vulnerable and appealing. Her hair was caught back in a ponytail and she had put on some lipstick; and Otani surprised himself by thinking that she looked altogether more attractive that way.

"You can say that again." After the glutinous obsequiousness of her employer's moppings and mowings Otani found her plain speaking refreshing. He grinned, something he rarely did, and she at once bristled. "Something amusing you?"

"No, no. I was smiling because you remind me of my daughter."

"Really. And the daughter of this senior government official is a wage slave too, no doubt?"

"In a way. She's a first-year student as a matter of fact, but she does have a side job as a waitress in a coffee bar."

Noriko looked taken aback by the ease with which Otani parried her sarcasm, and he pressed his advantage. "What's more, she thoroughly disapproves of my profession. She tells me I'm helping to prop up a corrupt political order."

"She sounds like an intelligent person."

"Oh, she is. Not always right, mind you, but intelligent and articulate. So I hope you don't feel insulted that you put me in mind of her. I get the impression that you don't approve of policemen either."

"What makes you think that?"

"Well, you know why I'm here, of course. So naturally I've already been asking a few questions. Patrolman Higashida thought you'd almost certainly have your own ideas about the murder but doubted if there was much prospect of your cooperating."

"He did, did he? Typical." Otani was gratified to notice her heightened color. "Then I suppose he also told you that I'm a progressive, and you jumped to the same conclusion as him."

"Sorry, I don't know what you mean."

"I mean that the pair of you automatically assume that a progressive hasn't got any common sense. I agree with your

24

daughter. I do think our society is rotten. But it doesn't follow that whoever murdered Craig Kington should get away with it."

"Good. I'm glad we've cleared the air. I mustn't detain you now, but I'd appreciate a private word with you some time tomorrow if you could spare half an hour?"

"All right. Early afternoon would be best. Two-fifteen at the snack bar at the bus station."

"Excellent. I'll be there. A very quick question before you go. Do you know a man called Tadao Mori?" Otani studied the maid's face with interest and, since she hesitated, quickly took the impressively addressed envelope out of his folder and showed it to her. "I've never heard of him myself, but I've just been given this letter from him—his name's on the back. Haven't read it yet."

"Ah. Well, he's a lawyer. And a crafty one. I'm not surprised he's popped up so quickly. Look, I've got to go."

"Of course. Thank you, Miss Ito. Goodnight." Much as he would have liked to, Otani made no attempt to extract anymore that evening from Noriko. Staring at the door she closed hurriedly behind her, he tried and failed to make up his mind whether she was embarrassed or frightened. Then he switched off the overhead light and settled himself cross-legged on the futon to study the letter and the contents of the file.

Kington's body had been found in the precincts of the Inari Shrine by a regular early worshipper there: the semiretired proprietor of a thriving hardware shop who attributed the success of the business to his diligent support of the shrine. The old man was well known and much respected in the locality for his public spirit, often putting on a green and white armband and seeing children safely across the road outside their primary school. He also turned out regularly for neighborhood fire drill, and all in all was, according to Higashida, a thoroughly reliable if loquacious witness.

The multiple stab wounds described by the medical examiner indicated a frenzied attack with a sharp knife, but the photographs showed that the body had been arranged in an attitude of apparent repose. In the doctor's opinion this must have been done immediately after death.

The elderly witness had, Higashida reported, seemed distressed not so much by the experience of stumbling upon a corpse as by what was in its hands. This, Otani could see from the pictures, was a small ceramic image of a luxuriantly bushy-tailed fox, of the type commonly sold as souvenirs at Inari shrines all over the country. It was certainly an odd thing for a murderer to leave in such circumstances—after wiping it clean of all fingerprints save those of the dead man.

Higashida had been to see Kington's partner Gary Wilson to tell him of the death and ask him to notify his superiors in Tokyo: Otani's own department had been in touch with the American consular authorities in Kobe. Reading Higashida's report Otani noted with relief that he said Wilson spoke Japanese with remarkable fluency. Wilson—who had not been told about the peculiar disposition of the body—claimed to be unable to suggest why anyone might be ill-disposed toward his partner. He had provided a list of the names of people who had been taking English lessons from Kington since they had arrived in Sumoto, but pointed out that in pursuing their mission they both took every opportunity to get into conversation with local people. Kington had therefore unquestionably made other Japanese acquaintances during their time there.

Otani blinked, rubbed his eyes and yawned. He had absorbed as much as he could for one day and needed to sleep on his impressions. It was still too early to go to bed, so it looked like a toss-up between the color television set near the *tokonoma* alcove and the book Hanae had slipped into his bundle. The TV was coin-operated and he doubted if he would watch it for the two hours a hundred yen would buy him. All the same he chose it as the less demanding option.

The color was still something of a novelty, and forcing thoughts of murder to the back of his mind he debated with himself whether some of his forthcoming summer bonus might be well spent on replacing their own old black and white set at home. For all Akiko's withering scorn about consumerism she had, according to Hanae, mentioned more than once that most of her friends' homes boasted all of the "three Cs" middle-class families currently aspired to: car, cooler and color.

The Otanis possessed none of these symbols of success. One national and two private railway lines provided frequent commuter services between the suburb of Rokko where they lived and central Kobe where he was based and Hanae did her serious shopping, the Hankyu Line station being no more than ten minutes' walk from the house. The Kobe University campus was about the same distance away up Mount Rokko in the opposite direction: a stiff walk but nothing to an eighteen-year-old. Otani disliked driving, and could no more imagine Hanae at the wheel of a car than at the controls of an airplane. As for air-conditioning, well, it could get hot and sticky for a few weeks in the summer, but their old house was well up on the hillside and there was usually a light breeze of an evening when it was most appreciated.

Nevertheless, color TV was a clear possibility, Otani reflected as he watched a mournful drama about the selfless wife of a dedicated teacher. She was dying of cancer, and urging her doctor to hasten her passing so that her inevitably distracting obsequies could be got out of the way during the school vacation. Otani found the plot less than gripping, so he tried another channel and was rewarded with the sight of a family from the provinces competing in a talent show. The aged, toothless grandmother who sang a current hit song with great élan was worth watching, but neither her middle-aged son nor his wife had any discernible skills and the numerous grandchildren were pudding-faced and ill-favored.

The only other program was a re-run of an old "Surprise Show" in which a contestant was hammering six-inch nails into a block of wood with his forehead. Otani sighed as he switched off and reached for the little package they had put with his yukata and towel. It contained a disposable toothbrush already impregnated with paste and a throwaway plastic razor. Pottering along to the large sink equipped with two cold-water taps at the end of the corridor he cleaned his teeth, then used the nearby facilities—euphemistically labeled "honorable hand-wash"—which were no more than average malodorous.

As he emerged he could hear raised voices downstairs. One was undoubtedly Suekawa's, though he was using crude language very different from the unctuous style he had inflicted on Otani earlier. The other could only have belonged to the crone he had spotted when he first arrived at the inn, peeping at him from inside the bathroom. From what Higashida had told him on the way, he realized that she must be Suekawa's mother, and though he had yet to see her properly he pictured her as being like the ancient he had recently been watching on television.

Not that she was singing in a cracked but merry voice well primed with sake: on the contrary, though Otani could make out very little she seemed to be giving her son as good as she was getting. After a while he shrugged and went back to his room, glanced once more through the photographs taken at the scene of the murder and then inserted himself between the futons with Agatha Christie for company.

Whether because of a peculiarity of the inn's acoustics or because the old lady and her son had stopped rowing it was very quiet in the room and Otani realized that he really was very drowsy. He did no more than riffle through the book, gathering that Hercule Poirot seemed to have got himself involved in some way at a girls' school in England, but was struck by one fragment of dialogue in which one of the girls was explaining something to the great sleuth. "It's about some murders and a robbery and things like that," she was saying earnestly, and Otani thought that a very appropriate point at which to close the book, switch off the bedside light and settle down to sleep.

Otani rarely dreamed, and when he did he usually enjoyed the experience as something of a treat. Not this time. In fact he woke suddenly in a panicky sweat, having been dangling from a precipice hanging on for dear life to a young woman who was either Noriko the maid or Akiko his daughter. Whoever it was, she seemed less than enthusiastic about hauling him up to safety, even though surely she could see the animals below, baying for his blood.

After a while he felt calmer. There was in fact a dog howling outside, somewhere not far from the inn: a most unusual sound in a Japanese town in the middle of the night and quite enough to trigger off a bad dream as well as a rash of complaints from its owner's irate neighbors. Especially this particular howling, strangely hoarse and somehow *knowing*. Even now that he was thoroughly awake it was not only annoying but unnerving, and a relief to Otani when he heard a door rattle open somewhere and a woman's voice which seemed to soothe the creature at once. He decided to have a cigarette, and smoked about two-thirds of it before stubbing it out and abandoning himself again to sleep, this time blessedly dreamless.

Chapter 4

"**I**NDEED IT IS. MORE LIKE APRIL THAN FEBRUARY." It wasn't until he had opened the shoji screens on getting up that Otani had realized his window faced east and that it was a beautiful morning.

"Are you quite sure you wouldn't have preferred a Japanese-style breakfast?" Mrs. Suekawa asked, looking dubiously at the two great doorsteps of buttered toast she had placed on the table with a pot of bright red jam, a jar each of instant coffee and "Creap" brand powdered milk substitute, with enough wrapped sugar cubes to sweeten gallons. The hot water was in a thermos jug with a flower design.

"Quite sure, thank you. I always eat Western-style food for breakfast. Like the Emperor, you know." The excellent meal of the previous evening had encouraged him to hope for something a little more sophisticated, but Otani forbore to add that the Imperial Palace probably ran to bacon or ham and eggs and proper coffee, just as Hanae provided at home. Not that it mattered much: anything was better than a raw egg, a pickled plum, miso soup and rice first thing in the morning.

It had been pleasant to watch Mrs. Suekawa briskly put away the bedding and set the room to rights while he sat in the little balcony area. It was only to be expected that at that hour she would be in Western dress, though he had the impression that she had nevertheless taken a good deal of trouble over her appearance. The brown woolen skirt was neat and fashionably short, revealing legs any Japanese woman of her generation might well be pleased to show off. The maroon color of her sweater was entirely suitable for a married lady, though Otani wasn't sure that he would have liked to see Hanae in public in one so close-fitting or without a cardigan over it. It was difficult for him to keep his eyes off Mrs. Suekawa's clearly defined breasts, and disconcerting that she was obviously well aware of the fact.

He cleared his throat noisily as he got up and went over to the table. "Well, thank you again. And for the newspaper. I'll glance through it while I have my breakfast, then I must be off. I expect to have a busy day." Judging from the warmth of her smile as she left Mrs. Suekawa was not offended by her clearly implied dismissal, and Otani banished thoughts of her bosom from his mind as he made himself a cup of coffee and attacked his toast.

The distracting bulges under the sweater were, however, again in evidence as she saw him off at the entrance, taking her time over murmuring the customary courtesies and stressing several times that the bath would be ready for his use at whatever time he returned. Otani had rather hoped that the old woman might have been about so that he could get a proper look at her, but there was no sign either of her or her obsequious son. He and Mrs. Suekawa had the small lobby to themselves, but in spite or perhaps because of this she stood, warm and perfumed, very close to him before finally sinking to her knees in respectful farewell.

Having escaped at last, Otani headed in the direction of the Inari Shrine. It was a little before eight, and Sumoto was beginning to come to life. A man in an ordinary jacket and the bottom half of a tracksuit was hauling bundles of newly delivered magazines and comics into the dark interior of a bookshop-cum-pharmacy, and a little further along a yawning girl was opening up a coffee shop called "Florida." It advertised a morning bargain service of a hard-boiled egg and half a banana with a cup of coffee at only fifty yen over the price of the coffee alone, and Otani was briefly tempted to drop in, but he manfully averted his eyes and soon came to the orangey-red *torii* gateway which marked the entrance to the Inari Shrine precincts.

He had expected the shrine to be modest in size and rather run-down as such places tended to be in minor provincial towns, largely neglected except on a few festival days a year. He was wrong. This one had grounds extensive enough to accommodate a kindergarten building complete with its own little playground on one side of the outer precinct, and a parking area for about a dozen cars on the other. A large, durable-looking white banner bore a boldly brushed notice claiming that the shrine was renowned for bringing health and prosperity to individuals who paid their respects there, and that special services were arranged on request to ensure a successful future for new businesses, and to purify new cars so as to guarantee their safety on the roads.

As Otani was studying this announcement the engine of one of the three cars in the parking lot roared into life, sending half a dozen pigeons clattering into the air. The driver was obviously in a hurry, because the car shot out of its slot, accelerated through the gateway and slewed with a squeal of tortured rubber into the road beyond so quickly that Otani barely had time to register before it disappeared that it was a new Mazda and that its sole occupant was a middle-aged man. It occurred to him that only its having been well and truly blessed at the shrine could have justified such reckless driving.

He continued his inspection of the grounds, which were well, even excessively, cared for, though he didn't care for the obtrusive soft-drink vending machine near the parking lot. The sanctuary area was about as large again as the outer precinct where he was standing, and at a level about four feet higher. Otani ambled up the broad flight of stone steps, pausing to admire the pair of fine stone fox images which stood guard over another, smaller torii gate. The whole inner area was symbolically fenced off with richly lacquered rails of the same orangey-red, and several fine mature trees marked the rear boundary.

The shrine proper comprised the usual scatter of buildings, to Otani's eye all in an impressive state of repair. In front and slightly to one side of him was a fair-sized shrine office with many windows. These were presently closed, but would, he knew, be opened up at appropriate times for the sale of talismans, picture postcards and fortunes, and also to enable people to book the services of the priest or priests for special rituals. Judging by the size of the place, Otani thought it probable that the staff also included a few shrine maidens, at least on a part-time basis. To his right was an elevated roofed stage where they could perform their grave ritual dances.

The bright morning sunlight gleamed on the lavish gilding of the lacquered columns supporting the massive but gracefully curved roof of the main sanctuary. Some eighteen inches thick, the material of the roof might have been taken at first sight for thatch but consisted in fact of layer upon layer of laminated bark strips, their exposed edges gentled by drifts of green, yellow and gray lichen.

At one side of the approach to the huge offertory box and the partially veiled entrance to the holy of holies was a plain wooden fence against which were stacked about thirty or forty sake barrels with the brewers' trade names prominently displayed, while on the other dozens of little wooden votive tablets were fastened to a large board. Otani glanced at one or two of the more recent petitions, inscribed with felt-tipped pens in immature calligraphy. A girl called Keiko begged for success in the forthcoming senior high-school entrance examinations, while Yutaka wanted gigs for his newly founded pop group.

Otani opened his file and took out the photographs. Two of them taken from different angles showed him clearly where the American's body must have been lying: to the left of the sanctuary enclosure, a yard or two back on a pathway leading past three mini-shrines toward the back boundary wall. Though the spot would be in plain view of anyone approaching the sanctuary it was nevertheless shaded by trees and relatively secluded.

Otani stood there pondering for two or three minutes before taking in the larger context, and particularly the new-looking detached private house which stood in its own plot to the other side of the path. Being inside the precincts of the Inari Shrine it was almost certainly the home of the priest. It was not only partially concealed behind high plastered walls but also well protected, as Otani discovered as soon as he drew near to the barred gate and a dog chained to a kennel outside the front door set up a furious barking. The racket momentarily recalled to his mind the weird, disturbing sounds of the night before and he stopped in his tracks, unreasonably perturbed. His unease was short-lived, though, because almost at once the front door of the house slid open and a woman appeared, silencing the dog with a quiet word as if by magic.

"Can I help you?"

"I'm so sorry to disturb you," Otani said through the bars.

"Come in, do. It isn't locked."

Otani opened the gate and took a couple of steps forward on a path flagged with handsome natural stones, but prudently remained beyond range of the chained dog, which was eyeing him in an unfriendly way. "I was looking for the priest."

"This is his house, but I'm afraid he's just left." There was nothing remarkable about the woman's appearance. She was wearing a cross between an apron and an overall, and a scarf was loosely tied over her hair: seemingly a lady who tackled her housework with vigor. She wore no make-up, but her complexion was smooth and fresh. Having so recently been all too aware of Mrs. Suekawa's physical charms Otani momentarily wondered if he might be turning into a sex maniac, for he found this woman most attractive, too. He judged her to be a few years younger than Mrs. Suekawa: in her early thirties probably. What struck him particularly about her as she went on was her low-pitched, beautifully modulated speaking voice. "You've missed him by about ten minutes."

Otani bowed, and then fished in his pocket for one of his name-cards which he offered to her. "What a shame. It must have been your husband I saw driving out of the shrine a while ago. Please allow me to introduce myself. My name is Otani, on temporary attachment to Sumoto police headquarters.''

The woman's eyebrows lifted as she studied the card. "*Inspector* Otani, I see. Head of criminal investigation at prefectural headquarters. My word, we are honored. We were a bit surprised that nobody from the police came to see us on the day . . . it happened. Or yesterday. You've certainly made up for it now though, haven't you? My husband will be sorry to have missed such an important visitor but I'm afraid he won't be back until tomorrow. Oddly enough, he's going to Kobe, where you've come from. I'm Naomi Horiuchi, by the way. Is there anything I can do for you?''

"Thank you, Mrs. Horiuchi, but not at the moment. We shall, if we may, put a few questions to both you and your husband within the next couple of days, but as you see I'm alone at the moment and I can't take a formal statement without an assistant to witness it. About what time do you expect him back tomorrow?''

She shrugged. "I can't say for sure. He always takes the car over, so that cuts down the number of possibilities. I can never see the point of it myself. The passenger ferries are much more frequent. Anyway, I can't see him getting back before mid-afternoon, and if he misses that one it'll be more like mid-evening.''

"Ah. Well, it might have to wait till the day after tomorrow, then. Would it be convenient for me to call back later today for your own statement, madam? Just a formality.''

"Yes, if you like. Preferably before my son gets back from school at about three-thirty, though.'' She smiled. "He's eight, and something of a handful.''

"I can well believe it. Good. I'll try to get back late this morning, but if that's not possible, would tomorrow morning at, say, nine be all right?''

"Whatever suits you best.''

Given the fact that the news of the murder of Craig Kington was all over Sumoto and that it had taken place within twenty or thirty yards of her own house, Mrs. Horiuchi was remarkably composed, Otani decided, after taking his leave of her. Especially as she had been one of the dead man's pupils, according to the list of names supplied by Gary Wilson.

Chapter 5

T HERE WERE ALL THE PREDICTABLE THINGS: A FEW KEYS on a holder with a leather tab indicating that it had been bought at the Tokyo Tower as a souvenir, a half-empty, crumpled, pocket-sized packet of paper handkerchiefs, an open pack of Lotte chewing gum with two sticks left in it, and loose change amounting to three hundred and seventy-seven yen. Otani shoved them to one side of the desk-top and turned his attention to the wallet taken from the body of Craig Kington. This contained more money: two five-hundred and three thousand-yen notes. It was a reasonable enough sum for an ordinary person to carry about. Otani normally had about that much on him, though he had brought much more to Awaji to cover his expenses, and Hanae who was in charge of the family budget always kept twenty or thirty thousand in the house so as to be able to deal with the various bill-collectors.

The wallet, which was of good-quality leather and looked fairly new, had several compartments and Otani emptied it out completely. He gave the alien registration card only a cursory glance, having already seen a photocopy of the relevant page of the register. The bearer's photograph could as usual have been of almost anyone. All Western males fell into one of two categories so far as Otani was concerned, the hairy hippies and the clean-shaven businessmen or the better-off, usually middle-aged or elderly tourists he saw with their wives in the smarter parts of downtown Kobe.

There were a few of Craig Kington's own name-cards, printed in English on one side and Japanese on the other. He had phoneticized his name as *Kureigu Kinguton* and described himself as a teacher of English. Of more interest was the small collection of other people's cards the American had stuffed away, and Otani jotted down the names and descriptions for future reference. Finally there were two photographs to consider.

One of these, obviously taken in America, showed a middle-aged couple he presumed to be Kington's parents. The other was a Polaroid instant snap which Otani studied with much interest before tucking it away in his own wallet and putting all the other items in a fresh envelope. Having stuck down the flap, he took his personal seal in its little leather case from his pocket, pressed it into the tiny pad of sticky red ink in its own ivory container at the end and made the OTANI impression across the join.

Then he turned to the bundle of clothing the dead man had been wearing, but didn't remove it from the clear plastic bag in which it had been stored. He was no forensic scientist and it would yield up whatever information it might harbor only to the experts. The little ceramic fox was another matter. That had been placed in a separate plastic bag. He had been assured it carried only Kington's fingerprints, but Otani didn't handle it, contenting himself by looking at it from every angle for a long time.

Eventually he stretched his arms, yawned and stood up. The office to which he had been shown on arrival at police headquarters well before nine-thirty had, it seemed, been placed at his disposal on the instructions of Inspector Takada, of whom there was no sign. Higashida was, however, already very much available, natty in a sports jacket and gray trousers. It was a pity about the hair, but otherwise he looked unobtrusively smart. Otani gave him the material he had been examining to put back under lock and key. Questioned about the personal items, Higashida earnestly assured him that they had been untouched since he personally removed them from the dead man's clothing and sealed them in the manila envelope. In fact they still had to be inventoried.

It was now nearly ten-thirty, and Otani drank down the remains of the cup of green tea a mumbling cleaning lady had brought him rather a long time earlier. He collected up the photographs which had been spread out on the desk, put them back in the folder of case notes he had been carrying about since the previous afternoon, locked it in the desk drawer and went downstairs to find Higashida waiting for him as instructed.

"There you are. Good. Now then, somewhere between my inn and the shrine earlier on I noticed a coffee shop called Florida. Would that be anywhere near this man's address?" Otani showed him the back of the envelope Tadao Mori had addressed to him, watching the young policeman's face as he studied it.

"Yes, sir, very near. No more than two or three minutes' walk away, I should think."

"Right. Let's go and have a cup of decent coffee, then. There are a few things I want to ask you. With a bit of luck the Florida morning service special goes on until eleven."

Ensconced a few minutes later at a tiny table in the coffee shop, Otani peered at Higashida as he shelled his hard-boiled egg. "You know who this Mori man is, then." It was a statement, not a question, and Higashida nodded. "Have a look at the letter." Otani handed it over and bit the top off his egg, then sprinkled salt on the yolk. He also had time to take a couple of appreciative sips of coffee before Higashida laid the letter down. "Finished? Good. You don't see lovely calligraphy like that so often these days. Anyway, rather mysterious, don't you think? All that business about sinister forces and ancient debts. I've learned already that Mori's a lawyer. What else can you tell me about him?"

"Not a lot, I'm afraid, sir. I've never met him, but I've had him pointed out to me so I know what he looks like."

"Ah. And what does he look like?"

"Um . . . well, old-fashioned, mainly, but I doubt if he's

sixty yet. Quite tall, but sort of dried-up. When I saw him he was wearing a Western suit and a shirt with a stand-up collar. And one of those cloak things with holes for the arms. I think they're called *inbaanesu*."

"I know what you mean. My father used to wear an Inverness. Anything else?"

"Only gossip, sir, though I'm pretty sure he's a widower. People might make fun of his appearance but everyone seems to be rather scared of him. They say he's a miser."

"Something of a recluse, is he? Doesn't get about much?"

"Oh no, quite the reverse, sir. He's the president of the Sumoto Historical Society and of the Awaji Folklore Research Group. Takes the chair at their monthly lecture meetings. Also judges the children's annual calligraphy competition. I can see why now."

"You seem to know a great deal about a man you've never met. He isn't also a communist, by any chance? Like your friend Miss Ito?" Otani regretted his last words as soon as they were out of his mouth and he saw their effect. "I'm sorry. You must forgive me, I have a bad habit of teasing people who can't answer back. In fact I had quite an interesting chat with Miss Ito last night, and it was she who told me Mori's a lawyer. Incidentally, it seems she's not averse to helping us after all."

"I know. I saw her later and she told me."

This rather shook Otani, and he took refuge in his coffee to collect his thoughts. When he spoke again he chose his words with greater care. "I see. Well, we've been thrown together in an unusual situation, you and I, and I think the best plan is for me to be as forthcoming as possible with you and hope you'll do the same by me. As you see, Mori claims to have information relevant to this case. Well, I'm going to drop in on him after we leave here and see what he's got to say for himself. Can I take it you have no idea what may be on his mind?"

"None whatever, sir. And I shouldn't think Miss Ito has, either. She thinks he's a busybody who likes to poke his nose into everything he can, but she didn't mention anything specific."

40

"But she shares the common opinion that there's something, how can I put it, slightly menacing about Mori?"

Higashida squirmed uncomfortably in his chair but eventually nodded. "I'd say so, yes."

"All right. As I expect she told you, we've arranged to meet at two-fifteen today for a chat. Now let's change the subject. I've already told you that I went and had a look round the Inari Shrine early this morning. What I didn't tell you is that I also had a short conversation with the priest's wife. He'd left for Kobe on some unspecified business and won't be back before tomorrow afternoon at the earliest. He was in a tearing hurry, too. I saw him go off in his car driving like a hot-rodder before I knew who he was. Anyway, Mrs. Horiuchi was very cooperative, and I'd like us to go together to get her formal statement before her husband returns. Probably tomorrow morning." Otani hesitated. He always preferred to play his cards very close to his chest, but something told him to keep his word to Higashida, at least over matters of fact.

"This next bit is strictly confidential. It may be nothing whatever to do with the murder, but I think there's something not quite right about the Horiuchis. She told me he was taking his car over on the ferry, so before I arrived at headquarters this morning I rang the prefectural vehicle registration bureau and got the number of the car. It's a new Mazda. Then I made another call, to divisional headquarters in Akashi. I thought it might be a good idea to have Horiuchi tailed from the ferry terminal to Kobe to find out the nature of his business there if possible. But of course we aren't going to let his wife know, are we?"

"No, sir. Obviously not." Higashida spoke in an awed whisper, overcome by his *de facto* promotion to the big league of criminal detection.

"Have *you* any thoughts about the Horiuchis? Before you answer that, did you notice either of them about while you were at the scene? You say the old man who found the body reported it to the nearest police box at six forty-three, and you arrived at the shrine at about seven-twenty."

"Yes, sir. I happened to be on the night shift and was

supposed to go off duty at seven. But when the caller came in I got some screens, the camera and other equipment together and went over to the shrine in the van at once. I posted the local man by the steps to stop anybody entering the inner shrine precinct and the driver and I had the body screened off by soon after seven-thirty. There didn't seem to be much point in trying to seal off the outer precinct too. Mothers bringing their children to the kindergarten probably noticed the police van but it would have attracted much more public attention if we'd tried to send them away. Mrs. Horiuchi came out of her house with her son to see him off to school just before eight. I intercepted them and told her briefly that there'd been an accident which we were investigating.''

''How did she react?''

''Quite reasonably. Concerned, but not particularly inquisitive. She explained that her son always made his own way to school and home in the afternoon, so I simply offered to see him out of the precinct for her. He had his name and address on a tag attached to his satchel so he'd be able to get back in easily enough, though it seemed unlikely the body would still be there in the afternoon. Mrs. Horiuchi said goodbye to the boy and went back into the house, I was able to steer him round the screens without too much trouble and off he went. The priest came out about half an hour later, in all his robes, black lacquer clogs, headdress and all.''

''And what was his reaction?''

''He totally ignored us, sir. It was extraordinary. The doctor had arrived by then and we'd opened up the screens to let him get at the body, but we might have been invisible for all the notice the priest took. He marched solemnly by without so much as a glance in our direction and went into the sanctuary. I know, because I followed him round the corner and watched.''

''Fascinating. You noticed of course that Mrs. Horiuchi's name was on the list of pupils the other American gave you?''

''Yes, sir.''

''So her original reaction, or lack of one, rather, suggests that she had no idea Kington had been killed. But she undoubtedly does now, and that's what puzzles me. You'd expect her to be upset to know that her teacher had been murdered practically on her doorstep, but her manner with me early this morning was entirely relaxed and matter-of-fact. What do you make of that, Higashida? Do the Horiuchis have any sort of reputation in Sumoto?'' Otani had long since dealt with his boiled egg and toast and now peeled the banana half which had been artistically cut in a deep zig-zag.

''The shrine itself is known to be very prosperous, and people talk about the *kannushi-san* as a go-getter. He was responsible for starting the kindergarten in the outer precinct a few years ago. I believe the fees are quite high. And the parking spaces are rented out by the month. The new regulation that you can't register ownership of a private car without proof of having somewhere off-street to keep it has made it very profitable to own a private parking lot anywhere in town.''

''Quite. And I see he offers all sorts of special rituals, including prayers for road safety and so forth. No doubt at a price. And all tax-free since it's a religious foundation, of course. Still, I must say he takes care of the place, so he must plough back a fair amount of the profits into maintenance work. Why do you smile?''

''Sorry, sir. It's just that he's very good at persuading local businessmen to pay for all that sort of thing. They get their names displayed prominently, and he's always ready to turn up to bless a new shop or restaurant. Then there's the monthly open-air market in the outer precinct. It used to be just a little local evening *ennichi*, a few stalls selling pots and pans, plastic toys, goldfish in bags, you know the sort of thing. You ought to see it now. In fact if you're still here on Friday you can.''

Otani's lip twitched, but he made no reply as he picked up their bill and took it to the girl at the cash desk near the door with Higashida in his wake. He said nothing until they were outside the shop, then looked at his watch.

''Right, this is what I'd like you to do. Take me to within sight of Mori's—what is it, house, office?''

''Both, sir.''

''Good chance he'll be there, then. All right, show me

where it is, and then I'd like you to go back to headquarters and get in touch with the other American. Tell him we'd both like to go and talk to him at home late this afternoon, say around four. I'm sorry to cut you out of the conversation with Mori but it isn't a formal interview, you see. He's asked to see me. By the way, it's up to you whether or not you sit in on my talk with Miss Ito this afternoon. If you choose to, I'll see you at the bus station. If not, back at the office by three-thirty."

Tadao Mori's home and office proved to be an impressive traditional wooden house, not unlike a smaller-scale version of the Tokiwa Inn in outward appearance. Alone at the entrance Otani studied the sign beside it which said simply "Tadao Mori, Attorney" and then tried to slide the door open in the usual way to announce himself. It was locked; something Otani would have found a little unusual at a private house and he certainly didn't expect at a place of business during normal office hours. There was, however, a bell push and Otani tried it. The bell seemed to sound a very long way away but it was distinctly audible and he waited patiently for a good minute for something to happen.

When it did it took him by surprise. He heard no approaching footsteps but all at once the door rattled open and a skinny hand and arm shot out, seizing Otani by the sleeve and pulling him in with surprising strength. A voice of indeterminate gender went with the arm. "Hurry, hurry! No time to lose!"

It seemed at first to be pitch dark inside and Otani stumbled and nearly fell as he left the bright sunshine. The door was closed behind him as abruptly as it had been opened, but after a few moments his vision adjusted itself to the gloom and he focused on the face of an elderly but spry-looking man in a black jacket, striped trousers and a wing collar. He was gazing at Otani with an expression of deep disapproval. "I have no telephone apparatus here, but it would," he said tetchily, "have been courteous to write a note. No, no, it's too late to apologize. Pray tell me immediately and without evasiveness what you know about the ancient province of Izumo."

44

Chapter 6

"**Y**ES, OF COURSE I'VE BEEN THERE. SEVERAL TIMES AS a matter of fact," Otani said defensively. He was still metaphorically in the dark, though his formidable host had not so much ushered as driven him into a study and into a chair that Mori cleared for him by the simple expedient of pushing all the books and files on it to the floor.

Otani had been in rooms like this before, usually occupied by professors of about the same vintage as his late father. The tatami matting of the floor had been largely covered by a threadbare carpet of an indeterminate color somewhere between red and brown, and papers protruded from the numerous pigeonholes of a huge roll-top desk which couldn't have been closed for years. The attorney was sitting with his back to it, in a massive old swivel chair that squeaked with his every movement. There were piles of books all over the floor, and bits and pieces of folk art and craft covered most other horizontal surfaces. The shoji screens over the window were closed and the room was as gloomy as it was stuffy, smelling of dust and, Otani rather suspected, brandy.

Tadao Mori seemed to have forgiven him for his lapse of good manners in not writing a note, but Otani was conscious that he was doing badly in his oral examination on the subject

45

of Izumo province, or Shimane Prefecture as he himself thought of it. Awaji was of course for administrative purposes part of Hyogo Prefecture which extended right across the main island of Honshu from Kobe to the Japan Sea side, and Izumo was up there too, but well to the west. Otani hoped that the lawyer would soon come to the point, if he had one, but he was interested enough in his personality to indulge him for a while.

"That's all very fine and large," Mori snapped. "But I'll warrant you know little or nothing of the Matsudairas."

A dim recollection of history lessons at school before the war drifted into Otani's consciousness. "Weren't they the feudal lords there in the old days?"

"Ah ha! We're getting there, we're getting there. Feudal lords, yes, and *a notorious fox-possessing family*. So there you are, you see." Mori rubbed his bony hands together, cracked his knuckles audibly and then sat back with a complacent, tight-lipped little smile, as though he had expertly led Otani through a long and complex chain of reasoning to some irrefutable conclusion.

"I'm sorry. I haven't the faintest idea what you're talking about."

Mori groaned theatrically, then sat up straight and smote himself on the side of the head. "Dear, dear, I must be getting senile. You may perhaps be forgiven. I omitted to mention the vital point, which is that Mrs. Suekawa senior of the Tokiwa Inn hails from Izumo, where her family were in the old days employed in various menial capacities in the Matsudaira household. *Now* do you understand?"

"No. Nor do I understand why you wrote to me." It was hardly courteous to be so blunt, but Otani was beginning to conclude that he was in the presence of a harmless madman, and that he could make better use of his time elsewhere.

Mori visibly made up his mind to try once more and leaned forward in a confidential manner. He smiled encouragingly at Otani, revealing a set of unnaturally large and regular false teeth. "*Think*, my dear Inspector. You seem to be a man of some innate intelligence, unlike the buffoon Takada to whom I have explained all this in vain. Think, and you will realize

46

that as is invariably the case, Mrs. Suekawa inevitably inherited her own family's fox-spirit and brought it with her to Sumoto. It is now comfortably installed with its regular quota of seventy-five dependants at the Tokiwa. Or perhaps I should say uncomfortably. You are in quest of a murderer, sir. Mark my words, the murderer is that fox.''

Otani had cultivated the control of his features for so many years that it had become rare for him to do so with a conscious effort. This was one of those times. The talk of fox-spirits and fox-possession was not in itself incomprehensible to him. Like all Japanese he had as a child been told stories of fabulous foxes who appeared in human form to bewitch, trick and on occasion do favors for people they took it into their heads to help. Sometimes in the old tales one assumed the guise of a beautiful woman who might even marry a poor man and bear him children; sometimes the form of a mysterious wanderer who would cheat an honest noodle or tofu seller out of his wares.

The thing that tended to give these disconcerting creatures away was the difficulty they had in preventing the tips of their bushy white tails from protruding from the bottom of their clothing; and of course their inordinate appetite for tofu plain or fried and for red beans cooked with rice. Otani even vaguely recalled having heard that in the old days certain families in country districts had been believed to harbor fox-spirits: a mixed blessing which could help them to prosper but could equally well lead to their being ostracized by their neighbors and finding their daughters virtually impossible to marry off, at least locally. But all that nonsense had long since been done away with.

"An interesting hypothesis, *sensei*," he said politely, breaking the silence which had prevailed for some time. "But I'm afraid I have to adopt a rather more practical line of investigation and I don't honestly expect fox-spirits to feature among the suspects."

"We shall see," Mori said calmly. Otani studied his face. Eccentric he undoubtedly was, but he didn't *look* crazy. Nor, once Otani had got used to his curious mixture of pedantry and economy with words, did he sound like a crackpot of

47

the kind who turned up often enough at police stations babbling about flying saucers or attempts on their lives by minions of the Emperor. Tadao Mori was obviously an educated man, and according to Higashida a solid, influential citizen and respected amateur scholar. Noriko Ito's reaction to the mention of his name had been to say the least of it wary. The eyes, too, were those of a man in full possession of his faculties.

"I have heard of so-called fox-possession," Otani admitted after a while. "But not since I was a child. Before people knew better, I suppose a mixture of autosuggestion and social prejudice might have made it seem real enough."

"A typically glib remark from a man too young to have avoided the materialist infection. I do not blame you, Inspector," Mori added charitably. "I on the other hand have made a close study of such phenomena, and I can assure you that you are on the wrong track. You have by now visited the Inari Shrine where the young man's body was found?"

"I have, yes."

"Yet, in spite of this, the significance of the *place* where murder was done—and bloody murder at that, I understand—escapes you?"

"Blood. Oh, I see what you mean. Pollution according to Shinto ideas."

"Precisely. There are to this day a number of shrines up and down the country where you may see notices forbidding entrance to women who are menstruating. How much more sacrilegious the deliberate, criminal spilling of blood in such a place! But you are still obtusely missing the real point, which is that while Shinto recognizes countless different tutelary deities, ours is an *Inari* shrine. Dedicated to which god?"

"Inari, obviously. The rice god."

"You are not totally uninformed, I am relieved to note. I pass over the fact that many scholars argue that there never was any such deity properly so called but that Inari was conjured out of the imaginations of illiterate peasants who had never studied the *Record of Ancient Times*. It is more than enough for our purposes that the god, or goddess, Inari has

48

for centuries been firmly established in the pantheon. And who, my dear sir, are the messengers and retainers of Inari? Ah! I see the light of dawn in your eyes. Of course! Foxes!''

Otani saw again in his mind's eye the pair of stone foxes at the shrine's torii gateway, and the little image in Craig Kington's folded hands in the grisly photographs of his body. Could Tadao Mori know about that? Higashida did, of course, as did the police driver who had helped him that morning, the medical examiner and the fingerprint man—unless this specialist, like the photographer, proved to be the ubiquitous Higashida in yet another role. Mori had, he claimed, tried out his preposterous theory on Inspector Takada, who had obviously preferred not to listen; though he might have mentioned the curious presence of the fox image in the dead man's hands to Mori if Higashida had told him about it. Probably not, though. Takada wanted to keep well clear, and Otani was beginning to conceive a certain sympathy for his point of view.

As for Mori, it would have been simpler for Otani if he were a straightforward crackpot, but unfortunately he had to admit that his wild mish-mash of ideas had opened up a few possibilities worth pursuing. That there might be some connection between the place of the murder and the little fox image he had to accept. Some crude attempt, perhaps, to throw suspicion on the priest Horiuchi or his wife, both of whom had some explaining to do. The rest was a farrago of nonsense, and it was time he had made that clear to the man.

''Mori-sensei,'' he said in a quiet, reasonable way. ''You are a lawyer. As such, even if in your practice you are concerned more with civil than with criminal cases, you have a better idea than most of police procedure. You are also a prominent citizen of Sumoto and a respected scholar. Do you, a highly educated man, seriously expect me to return to Kobe and report to my superiors and to the district prosecutor that in my opinion this young American missionary was murdered by one or more fox-spirits unknown, for reasons unknown, but possibly on behalf of the god of rice?''

''Not unknown, Inspector. Oh dear, no. I've already made

that clear. The fox concerned belongs to the Suekawa family, and the foreigner must have caused it grave offense.''

That did it. The man was obviously unhinged, and it was time to go. Mori made no attempt to stop him beyond vaguely suggesting that Otani might care for some refreshment, a cup of tea perhaps. Otani declined, to Mori's manifest relief, and a couple of minutes later Otani was once more outside the front door, blinking in the bright sunshine.

He checked the time and wondered briefly whether it might be worth going back to the shrine to interview Mrs. Horiuchi formally, but then decided that it would be preferable to wait until he had heard from divisional headquarters in Akashi. They should have had no trouble in spotting Horiuchi's car as it came off the ferry and tailing him, but it remained to be seen whether there would prove to be any profit in it. At all events, the more he had been able to find out about the priest by the time he spoke to the man's wife again the better.

Otani looked around and sniffed the fresh, unseasonably mild air. He had a lot to think about: an almost embarrassingly rich haul of ideas and impressions considering he had not yet been a full twenty-four hours in Sumoto. He decided to let them mingle at the back of his mind until it was time to meet Noriko Ito at the bus station at two-fifteen and to enjoy the sunshine while strolling round the town to orient himself properly, finding himself some lunch in the process.

His explorations didn't amount to much. Sumoto struck him as being a pleasantly compact little place, nestling as it did among low, wooded hills. One area away from the center was clearly the heart of the so-called hot-spring resort. It boasted half a dozen inns none of which seemed to Otani to be anywhere near the standard of the Tokiwa, a couple of bars and a shabby little cinema specializing in "pink" films. Judging by the posters outside, its current offering featured gangsters in sharp suits and dark glasses leering at girls naked to the waist and tied by the wrists and ankles to various items of furniture in a luxury flat, while the following week's attraction showed what looked suspiciously like the same cast doing much the same thing in, or in the case of the girls largely out of, traditional samurai costume.

Otani passed police headquarters again and located the bus station, near the municipal offices. Very few buildings were of more than two storeys, even in the center of town, though he noticed one large and impressive private medical and surgical clinic which looked as if it had been built very recently. There weren't too many of those about in the sixties, even in much bigger Japanese cities.

Sumoto seemed to have only one shopping street of any consequence, a straight thoroughfare two or three hundred meters long lined with mostly untidy, splendidly cluttered, open-fronted shops, with a few more substantial businesses among them. The Mitsubishi Bank had a branch there, as did the Hyogo Trust Bank. Against the background provided by such comparatively glossy premises a few old women were peddling fish, vegetables and fruit at the roadside, and the plain, honest smells of their wares reminded Otani that he hadn't had what he thought of as a proper meal since early the previous evening.

Briefly tempted to drop in at a sushi bar that looked inviting, he took a second look at the prices displayed in its little window and decided to have a bowl of noodles at a cheap eating-house nearby instead at a quarter of the cost. The place was on the rough and ready side but perfectly clean, and when he went in he was greeted with a cherry shout of welcome. A handwritten poster on the wall listed a good half-dozen different noodle meals, both Chinese and Japanese. Otani generally preferred fat white *udon* to the thinner brown buckwheat *soba* and more often than not chose the popular topping of pieces of chicken breast and sliced spring onions. Yet, when the middle-aged waitress came to take his order, he asked for *kitsune udon*, or fox noodles, almost without thinking. It seemed appropriate, somehow, since foxes had so dominated his curious conversation with Tadao Mori.

Within a minute or two the waitress placed a huge, steaming bowl in front of him and Otani reached for a pair of disposable chopsticks from the container on his table. He had been given a generous helping indeed: plenty of noodles in a broth with an appetizing smell, surmounted by quite a little mountain of strips of deep-fried bean-curd. He picked

51

one up with the chopsticks and chewed it thoughtfully, enjoying its slightly rubbery texture but struck for by no means the first time by the fact that tofu didn't really taste of anything much at all. Odd that foxes were reputed to be so fond of it that the dish had been named after them.

And even odder that spectacular murder should have been done in such a sleepy little backwater as Sumoto. But then Sumoto had already produced a number of surprises: an unusually enterprising and versatile young policeman, an inn numbering among its staff a talented cook, a hostess of mature but undeniably seductive charm and a touchy but lively-minded communist maid, a police chief who had to all intents and purposes already pensioned himself off, a mad lawyer raving about magical foxes and a cultivated young mother seemingly unperturbed by a violent death more or less on her premises.

Otani finished his fox noodles, slurping the last of the broth straight from the bowl, wiped his mouth with his handkerchief, paid and left the humble *shokudo*, wondering if the afternoon ahead could possibly be as interesting as the morning had been.

Chapter 7

"**H**AVE YOU TOLD HIM ABOUT MORI'S IDEAS?**" Noriko demanded with a glance at Higashida who had his back to them and was moodily leafing through one comic book after another which he took from the rack beside the kiosk fifteen yards or so away from the bench on which they were sitting. The woman in charge of the kiosk was glaring at the browser balefully but made no serious attempt to stop him. Somewhat to Otani's surprise Higashida had turned up at the bus station a little before two-fifteen, only to be briskly banished to a distance by Noriko when she herself arrived, in her jeans and sweater, a few minutes late.

"No, there wasn't time before you shooed him away. Why don't you want Higashida in on this conversation? Sooner or later I might have to ask you to make a formal statement, and if I do I'll need him to witness it."

"What I know for sure is one thing and I don't mind it going on record if and when it has to. What I may or may not think is something else entirely, and nothing to do with him." In order to break the ice and get her talking Otani had given her a heavily edited account of his conversation with Mori, saying nothing about his obsession with foxes but mentioning that he had spoken darkly about odd goings-on in the Suekawa family. Remembering Noriko's reaction to the mention of Mori's name the previous evening he had half expected her to try to change the subject, but she was reasonably forthcoming. She explained that Mori was well known for airing his views about a number of local families to whom for one reason or another he had taken a dislike, and seemed to be unsurprised by his prejudice against the Suekawas.

"All right. It's what you think that interests me most at the moment anyway. But I can't very well avoid taking whatever you tell me into account when Higashida and I are discussing this case. I'll have to try not to be too specific. Tell me, do you think there's anything odd about the Suekawa household? You live in at the Tokiwa, I presume?"

"You presume wrong. I did live in for a few weeks when I first started there last year, but now I've got a room nearby in a house where a couple of comrades of mine live. My own family aren't far away in any case, less than half an hour by bus. I often go there on my day off."

"I see. Mind my asking why you stopped living in?"

'Yes, I do mind." Noriko's tone was laconic but something in her expression made Otani visualize the oily Suekawa making crude overtures to her, even perhaps forcing his way into her room.

"Let me repeat my previous question, then. Mori seems to think there's something a bit, well, sinister about the Suekawas. Strictly between ourselves, I think he's well on the way to being off his head, but what's your opinion?"

Otani had already decided that it must be something of an effort for Noriko to look sullen most of the time, and he greatly enjoyed both the smile that briefly transformed her face and her suppressed giggle. "He must have been going on about the old girl and her tofu. He's convinced she's some kind of witch."

"And you obviously aren't."

"Of course not. She's daft all right, but quite harmless."

"Tell me about the tofu."

"Nothing much to tell. She nicks it from the kitchen when she thinks nobody's watching and puts it out the back at night. For the fox and his family, she says. No foxes around here, needless to say. Whenever her son catches her at it they have a fine old row. He calls her an extravagant old witch wasting good food, and she shouts back that it's only the foxes that keep the place going.''

''How in the world would Mori know about something like that?''

''He makes it his business to know all sorts of things about all sorts of people. You're much mistaken if you think he's off his head. For a start, he's one of the richest men in Awaji. He owns property all over the place and I dare say he'll own the Tokiwa too before much longer.''

''Are you serious?''

''Certainly I am. The Suekawas are up to their ears in debt to him. Look, I haven't got all that much time, you know. Don't you want to get to the point?''

''What particular point did you have in mind?''

''Well, stop me if I'm wrong, but I was under the impression you're here to investigate a murder. You seem to be asking questions about everybody except Craig Kington himself. Hasn't it occurred to you to wonder *why* somebody killed him?''

''Of course it has. As a matter of fact Higashida and I are going directly from here to talk to his colleague.''

''Gary Wilson. You won't get much out of him.''

''We shall have to see, shan't we? At least I'm told he speaks Japanese fluently. Anyway, I assure you I'm very interested in Craig Kington, so why don't you tell me about him? Better still, perhaps you'd tell me who killed him, and why?''

The look Noriko shot at him made Otani realize that he was handling her clumsily. Given what he had already learned of her attitudes and opinions, if he was to gain her confidence it was vital to avoid talking and behaving like a pompous bureaucrat, and to make it clear to her that he was capable of listening to her, taking what she said seriously and treating her like the rational, intelligent adult she was. He ought to be able to do that without unsuccessfully aping her own nat-

55

urally cheeky, throwaway style in a way she clearly found patronizing.

"Forgive me, Miss Ito," he said. "That was a thoughtless, condescending thing to say. If you can spare a little more time I should be truly grateful for your opinions."

She continued to look at him coldly for several seconds before her expression softened. "You're a strange man, aren't you? Higashida told me you apologized to him yesterday and seemed to mean it. He was staggered. And now it's my turn."

Otani shrugged, embarrassed. "Your own manner's a bit, well, disconcerting perhaps. And I talked down to you because I suppose you put me on the defensive."

"What, because I think they organize things better in North Korea?"

This time they smiled openly at each other, on equal human terms again. "Well, if you believe that you'll believe anything, I suppose, but even so I'd still like to hear from you about the American. You knew him?"

"Slightly. Soon after they arrived in Sumoto he and Gary Wilson turned up at a demo our group had organized to protest against the increased budget for the so-called self-defense forces. In fact it turned out that they'd come to argue with us, but in any case they could have been in trouble because the conditions of their visas don't permit foreigners to take part in political activity in Japan. So some of us warned them off, and the strong arm of the law over there joined in. He looks very fed up with those comics, by the way. I don't mind if you call him over." Higashida had been casting woebegone looks in their direction from time to time and he brightened and joined them with alacrity when Otani caught his eye and beckoned.

"Miss Ito has just been telling me you both first met Kingston and Wilson at a demo soon after they came to live in Sumoto. You were there to observe, I suppose?"

"Yes, sir. Plain clothes, of course—"

"But we all knew who he was, needless to say."

Otani looked from one to the other benignly, diverted by the thought that Noriko Ito was deemed by the authorities to be a potential subversive and that Patrolman Higashida—he

56

must find out his first name—was officially responsible for keeping an eye on her. How pleased he must be! For in the humdrum everyday setting of the bus station they looked what they really were: a young couple who were strongly attracted to each other but unsure of themselves, and ill at ease in the presence of the formidable stranger they probably thought old enough to be the father of either of them.

"So you warned the two Americans that it was against the immigration rules for them to be involved in a demo, but took no further action, right?"

"Yes, sir. It seemed unnecessary. They obviously understood what we were saying. The older one, Gary Wilson, argued a bit but after a minute or two they went off quietly enough."

Noriko took up the story. "A couple of days later Craig Kington turned up at the Tokiwa one morning, offering free English conversation lessons. Some tale about preparing ourselves for a big boost in foreign tourism once Expo 70 gets under way in Osaka. Considering that out of all the thousands of gaijin who went to the Tokyo Olympics in '64 not a single one got as far as Awaji so far as I know, I pointed out that the Tokiwa was hardly likely to be overrun with them the year after next. Then Mrs. S. came to find out what was going on. She obviously liked the look of him and the cute way he spoke Japanese. Next thing she was ushering him in and telling me to fetch tea and cakes. If anybody was going to be getting English conversation lessons at the Tokiwa it was obviously going to be her, not me."

Otani looked at Higashida. "Mrs. Suekawa's name isn't on that list of students Wilson gave you." Then he turned back to Noriko. "Did she in fact take lessons from him? After that first meeting, I mean?"

"Not at the Tokiwa, so far as I know. But she kept in touch with him."

"You're sure?"

"Quite sure. Because I did, too."

"*You* did?"

"Yes. Craig wasn't allowed to get involved with political activity, but there was no reason why he couldn't meet a few

57

of us once or twice a week socially to talk in English. He'd given me one of his name-cards and after talking it over with a few comrades I organized an informal discussion group. Meeting in various people's houses."

"Why on earth would a Christian missionary want to take part in something like that? Come to that, why would you and your friends want to talk to him?"

Noriko shrugged. "Progressives are internationalist. We like to keep in touch with comrades in other countries, read their journals, correspond, even hope to meet them if the opportunity arises. Most of us can read English, but it seemed a good chance to improve our skills and do something about the spoken language. Craig made no bones about his motives. He said he fully intended to convert us. We used to laugh at him. It really was a joke, because it was pretty obvious that what he really wanted to do was meet Japanese women and try to get them to go to bed with him."

Otani cast a sidelong glance at Higashida who had gone bright red and was looking deeply unhappy. He himself was taken aback by Noriko's candor, but had long since lost the capacity to be shocked by anything so banal as the phenomenon of male desire. "I'm afraid I don't really know anything about these Mormons," he said hesitantly, "but I seem to remember reading or hearing somewhere that their rules are particularly strict about that sort of thing."

"No, you're getting muddled up with stimulants," Noriko said calmly. "They aren't allowed to smoke, or drink alcohol, coffee or even tea. Not that Craig was particularly strict. He didn't smoke, but he certainly drank at our discussion meetings. As for sex, he tried to explain the Mormon attitude but I never did quite understand. He wasn't a priest, you know. No. It seems all young Mormon men have to spend a couple of years as missionaries either in America or some other country after they've finished their education, but after that they go home, get married and get a perfectly ordinary sort of job. Craig said Mormon men used to be able to have as many wives as they could afford, like in China or here in Japan in the old days, but it's against American law now. I suppose they make up for it by having mistresses instead, the way Japanese men do."

"Er . . . yes. Do you mind if we get back to Mrs. Sue-kawa? You said you were certain she kept in touch with Craig Kington, but not at the Tokiwa. Where else might she have met him? Not at your discussion group, surely?"

"That's a laugh. No, of course not. He and Gary Wilson shared a house. One of the rooms there is fitted up with wall charts and a projector and so on. Students could go there individually or in small groups."

"Higashida-kun, do you know if they had proper permission to operate a language school?"

Higashida had been lost in agonized speculation about the likelihood that Noriko Ito had been among the Japanese women Kington had tried to lure into bed and the possibility of her having succumbed; and Otani had to repeat the question before he understood it. Even then he didn't know the answer, and Otani made a mental note to raise the question with Gary Wilson later that afternoon. He turned back to Noriko. "Will you be at the Tokiwa this evening?"

"Yes. Between five and about eight or soon after."

"I'll hope to have another word with you then if possible, after we've seen Gary Wilson. You've pointed the way to a number of areas it might not have occurred to us to consider."

"I rather thought I might. See you, then."

"Thank you again—" but she was already on her way, a jaunty little figure disappearing round the corner, with Patrolman Higashida gazing after her with a wild surmise.

Chapter 8

"**A**ND IF YOU WANT MY OPINION," OTANI SAID RATHER tetchily, "she wanted you to know and it was less embarrassing for her to come out with it while I was there." He considered he had heard enough for the time being from Higashida about Noriko Ito. "You obviously didn't know as much as you thought you did about the people she's been associating with. Is this the place?"

"Yes, sir." The chastened Higashida had led Otani through a series of side streets and into what amounted to little more than a pathway between a rice and salt dealer's and a bicycle repair workshop. A ramshackle little wooden house had been squeezed into what had probably previously been the workshop's open yard, facing the blind wall of the living quarters attached to the rice shop.

"Plenty of privacy once you're inside," Otani commented. "On the other hand that old fellow in the rice shop probably notices everybody who comes and goes. It might be worth your having a chat with him some time in the next day or two. Also the bicycle man if you see him about, though he obviously doesn't live here."

"Yes, sir. The rice shop has a phone and they take messages for the Americans—for Mr. Wilson, I should say. The old man went and fetched him to talk to me when I rang this morning. We're a bit early, sir. He's not expecting us till half past three.''

A small bell styled like those at Buddhist temples hung outside the door of the house, a frayed piece of string hanging from its clapper. It produced a hollow clanking when Otani sounded it, and almost at once the door was opened and he found himself face to face with Gary Wilson.

Otani had met Westerners often enough before, some of them able to make themselves understood quite effectively in Japanese. Even so he never quite believed in their ability to speak his language, and though he had been assured that the tall young man at the door was unusually fluent it was nevertheless reassuring when he bowed politely and greeted them with all the proper courtesies. The American accent was perceptible, but as Wilson went on to invite them in and comment appropriately on the weather Otani's ear soon became adjusted to it.

Gary Wilson was not only tall but also thin, and he was dressed unobtrusively in a dark gray suit, a white shirt and a necktie of a nondescript blue not unlike that of the one Otani was wearing himself. His brown hair was cut short and neatly combed, his fingernails were well cared for, and he smelt strongly of disinfectant. The very ordinariness of his general appearance made his face the more interesting. It seemed unusually lined and careworn for a young man in his twenties, but what struck Otani most was its pallor. Wilson's skin was chalk-white and even his thin lips looked unnaturally pale. It might have been a death-mask, especially in view of the hospital aroma that hung about him, were it not for the American's glittering, toffee-brown eyes.

The interior of the house belied its tumbledown façade. There wasn't much room, but a complete absence of the clutter and accumulation of knick-knacks found in practically every Japanese home resulted in an effect of comparative spaciousness. In the tiny entranceway there was just enough room for Otani and Higashida to leave their shoes, and two pairs of felt slippers similar to those Wilson was himself wearing had been placed ready for them to step into.

The entrance gave directly on to the living room, which was obviously also where instruction was given. This was in more or less Western style, in that the floor was of shiny, pinkish-brown vinyl tiles and the walls were painted white, rather than plastered the usual dull brown.

There was a minimum of furniture: a square table with a surface of plastic veneer was surrounded by four straight chairs, and a single easy-chair stood in the far corner beside a low table on which there were a slide projector and two boxes of slides. The severity of the room was modified by the two red and gray striped rugs on the floor, and three brightly colored posters on the wall facing the door.

Gary Wilson settled his two visitors at the table, excused himself and disappeared briefly through a door at the back of the room. While he was gone Otani considered the posters, which were poorly executed and remorselessly educational. One showed the interior of an American kitchen and various items which belonged in it, such as bottles of milk and ketchup, cups and saucers, a tea-towel, a clock and so forth. The second was obviously designed to help students master the vocabulary of transport, the artist having contrived to squeeze into the improbable scene not only a bus, a train, a boat and a plane, but also bicycles and cars. The third featured agriculture: in the foreground a tractor, a cow, a sheep, a pig, and a number of hens in amicable proximity and in the background a barn and a stable with a horse peering out of it.

Wilson soon returned with three glasses of Calpis on a tray. Otani quite liked this well-advertised yogurt drink and sipped from his glass appreciatively as soon as Wilson invited him to. Then he apologized again for calling on him at comparatively short notice. "Especially in view of the fact that you have already been very helpful in providing information to my colleague here." Though he said nothing, Higashida visibly basked in the description of himself as a colleague. "Without wishing to intrude on your privacy at what must be a time of great distress, there are, I'm afraid, a number of points I must raise with you."

"I understand. I shall cooperate to the best of my ability."

"Thank you. I'm sure you will. Let me begin by just going over what you've already told us. You formally identified the body of Craig Kington at the hospital mortuary on the day it was found, but you last saw him alive during the afternoon of the previous day, Sunday. That is correct?"

"Yes. He went out just before I was due to receive two pupils here at five-thirty."

"And he didn't return during the course of the evening?"

"Presumably not, though I can't be sure."

Otani permitted his eyebrows to rise. "This is a small house. I should have thought it would be difficult for either of you to come or go without the other knowing."

"I apologize for not making myself clear, Inspector. After my lesson was over I myself went out for a meal. At a tempura bar. I got into conversation with the cook there and returned quite late. About nine, I suppose. Craig could have come and gone again during my absence, or, of course, after I had gone up to my room. I have a small television set there and with it on I wouldn't necessarily hear him come in."

"I see. But he definitely wasn't here at nine?"

"I'm almost sure of that much. He could have been sleeping, I suppose, but it's unlikely. He always kept much later hours than me."

"So would it be fair to say that until you heard what had happened you assumed that your colleague had returned to the house either while you were watching television or after you had gone to sleep?"

"Yes, that is correct."

Otani drank most of the rest of his Calpis and shifted in his chair. "You are entirely free to refuse, but I wonder if you would allow us to see over the rest of this house?"

Wilson stood up at once. "Of course. There's little enough to show you, but I have no objection. This way, please."

He led the way through the door at the back of the room. Beyond it was an area too short to be called a corridor but big enough to give access to a wooden staircase so steep that it was more like a ship's companionway. Edging past it, Wilson showed them a tiny but clean kitchen, equipped with little more than a sink with an electric water heater fixed to

63

the wall above, a shelf with a few pots and pans on it and a wall-mounted cupboard with sliding glass doors through which a modest collection of crockery could be seen. There was room for a table which offered little in the way of work surface, since it also accommodated a double electric cooking ring and a miniature refrigerator, as well as a packet of sugar, a jar of jam, a wrapped loaf and a large can of orange juice with two holes punched in the top.

"We don't—that is, I don't—do much cooking," Wilson said unnecessarily, then added, "I don't really care to with the toilet just the other side of that door."

Otani peeped in. It was at least a flush toilet, of the common trough type, and perfectly clean, though he thought it must be awkward for a tall man to use in such a confined space. "No bathroom, unfortunately, but there's a public bathhouse quite near," Wilson went on. "And a laundry." He backed out of the kitchen and put a foot on the first of the precipitous stairs. "Perhaps I should lead the way. Be careful, it's very steep."

He was quite right, and might well have added that there was no banister rail to hang on to. Otani had to kick off his slippers and sidle up crabwise in order to keep his balance, and Higashida followed his example. The upper floor of the house consisted of two rooms, one on either side of a narrow space at the head of the staircase. Wilson had slid open the door of the one above the kitchen and stood waiting for them inside. "This is where I sleep," he said. "The . . . the other bedroom is slightly larger, also Western-style. The whole house is Western-style."

It was not surprising that after dispensing with the felt slippers to climb the stairs Otani should find bare floorboards cold to his stockinged feet, but the chill seemed only fitting, for it was a spartan, comfortless little room. It contained a single iron bedstead that looked as if it had come from an institution, the sheets and blankets taut and flat round its thin mattress. There was a flimsy-looking clothes cupboard and a small desk with a plain wooden chair against the wall opposite the bed. On the desk Otani saw a plastic pen tray containing a few pencils and ballpoint pens, a newspaper and three books that he thought were almost certainly dictionaries. By the head of the bed was a side table; and on it a bedside lamp, a packet of paper handkerchiefs and another book, black, and this one bound in what looked like limp imitation leather. From one of a short row of hooks fastened to the wall near the door hung a navy-blue raincoat, while a precarious-looking shelf had been rigged up and somehow suspended from two of the others, to accommodate a small portable television set, its lead trailing across the floor to the one power point Otani could see, where it joined that of the bedside lamp in a multiple plug. And that, apart from a little green mat on the floorboards beside the bed, was all.

"You live very simply, Mr. Wilson," Otani said. "Practically like a Zen monk. But then you are a missionary, of course." Wilson did not respond and it occurred to Otani that he might have given offense by his reference to religion. "May we see Mr. Kington's room also, please?"

The American still said nothing, but Otani thought he saw his shoulders rise in an embryonic shrug as he gestured toward the door by way of inviting the two police officers to go ahead. Otani opened the door on the other side of the stairhead himself and stood very still for a moment before slowly entering Craig Kington's former domain.

The contrast was startling. Quite apart from having much better natural lighting because of being at the front of the house, the murdered man's room was comparatively speaking a luxurious mess. There was no iron bedstead, and the interior-sprung mattress placed directly on a fair-sized carpet that covered most of the floor area belonged to a Western-style double bed. Part of its label was visible, under a tumbled heap of pillows and eiderdowns.

An elaborate construction of box unit shelving had been built up against almost the whole of one wall. There were books in some of the boxes, clothes stuffed anyhow into others, and a radio and record player with twin speakers fitted in among them. The desk was larger than Wilson's, and its surface was a jumble of books and papers. Most eye-catching of all was a huge pin-up poster fixed to the wall. It showed a laughing blonde girl on a sunny shore, surf foaming round her golden thighs. She wore only the lower half of a bikini and a sodden T-shirt clinging to her breasts and erect nipples.

It was impossible to ignore the picture of healthy young animal glee and blatant sexuality, and Otani studied it for a while quite openly before glancing in turn at the others. Higashida had turned aside and was gazing in apparent fascination at the record player. Wilson remained just outside the door, an expression of acute distaste on his face. When their eyes met Otani spoke to him.

"Mr. Wilson. Have you been in here since . . . it happened?"

"I have never been in there."

Something about the American's face and his tone of voice convinced Otani that he was telling the truth, unlikely though it sounded. He made a quick decision. "It will be necessary for us to examine the contents of this room, which may contain evidence relevant to our inquiry. Mr. Kington's personal property will of course be handed over to the American consular authorities in due course, but when this officer and I leave here I propose to seal the room. You can no doubt provide me with a long strip of paper, or something which will serve?"

"I can, yes, but I see little point. Nothing would induce me to go into that room."

"I believe you, but that is not the only point to be considered. Officer Higashida, please remain here for a few minutes. May we have a word downstairs, Mr. Wilson?"

Wilson did not reply, but turned and began to negotiate the stairway, Otani following close behind. Back in the downstairs room Otani sat at the table and indicated the place opposite. The two men looked steadily at each other for a short time before Otani asked the obvious question.

"Tell me, did you hate Craig Kington enough to kill him?"

Chapter 9

OTANI DABBED HIS FOREHEAD, REFOLDED THE HAND-towel neatly and balanced it again on top of his head as he lowered himself once more into the welcoming depths of the bath. It was roughly oval in shape except for the straight end against the wall where the hot water tumbled out of a spout fashioned from rough stones, and faced with peacock-blue tiles which gave the water an exotic tint. The bath was about ten feet long and seven or eight feet across at its widest part, and when Otani stood upright on the bottom the water came up to the middle of his chest. Across the end of the oval there was a ledge about a foot high and deep enough to accommodate a couple of people sitting in comfort. Otani occupied it in solitary state, immersed to the chin and reflecting on the day's events, culminating in the visit to Gary Wilson.

He had not seriously expected the American to respond to his question by blurting out a detailed confession, but hoped rather to put him sufficiently off balance for him to make some slip of the tongue which would either tend to incriminate him or yield some other lead which could be followed up. The remarkable thing, he reflected as the hot water relaxed him, calming and ordering the turbulence of his ideas and impressions, was that even when Wilson grew angry and excited his command of Japanese did not desert him.

The American must have realized that after saying what he had through the open door of Kington's room there was no point in trying to disguise his antipathy toward his late partner. He could, however, have played it down, represented it perhaps as simple incompatibility between a man of strong religious principles and austere personal habits and a co-worker who must, to judge from the environment he had constructed for himself, have been sloppy, physically self-indulgent and far from dedicated to his missionary work. Wilson could reasonably enough have claimed that since he and Kington had not chosen each other as partners but been assigned to live and work together as the only Westerners in a remote country town they had inevitably, for both their sakes, had to arrive at some sort of agreement to keep out of each other's way outside working hours as far as it was physically possible to do so while sharing a house.

He did not. It was as though, having made a great effort to speak about Craig Kington in neutral terms when Otani and Higashida first arrived, he welcomed the chance to speak frankly. He freely admitted that he had detested Kington from the moment they had begun to work together, that he had lodged frequent complaints about him with the Tokyo headquarters of the Church of the Latter-Day Saints, and made repeated requests to his superiors to be reassigned. His tongue well and truly unlocked, he described Kington variously as a godless man and a damned soul doing the work of the Devil.

According to Wilson, Kington had been an insatiable lecher, a mocker, a blasphemer, a pervert, a clandestine communist, a betrayer of the teachings of his church, who bragged about drinking alcohol and jeered at the institution of the family and the American way of life. Wilson also mentioned other sins of which Kington had been guilty but some of them Otani couldn't remember and some he'd never heard of. He well remembered Wilson's glassy brown eyes, though, like windows behind which was a dreadful void, and the flecks of spittle that had gathered at the corners of his bloodless lips by the time he ended his diatribe.

"So you had reason to kill him?"

Wilson had blinked and shaken his head like somebody coming out of a daze as Otani put his question, then spoken in a quieter, more natural voice. "I wished him dead. I am glad he is dead. But I did not kill him."

Otani had left him sitting at the table when he went to join Higashida upstairs and they looked through Kington's belongings, putting the room more or less to rights as they did so. Most of the papers on the desk they scooped up and put in an empty holdall they found, for examination at leisure, with the contents of its two drawers. They found nothing of interest among the books or clothes, and by the time they had finished Otani had decided there really was little point in sealing the room.

It wasn't until the last minute and Higashida was halfway down the stairs with the holdall that Otani made his most significant find, not in Kington's room but in Wilson's. He couldn't think why he had taken it into his head to take a second quick glance round in there before going downstairs, but was very glad he had. It was a small ceramic image of a fox, and Otani found it in the rickety clothes cupboard, tucked inside a cheap pair of lightweight canvas shoes. He covered it carefully with a clean handkerchief before easing it out of the shoe and slipping it into his pocket.

"Gomen kudasai! Ojama itashimasu!" Otani had been completely lost in thought and was so startled by the rattle of the bathroom door being opened and the cheery mixture of greeting and apology that he almost slipped off his ledge and submerged. Regaining his sense of time and place he mumbled a perfunctory "Come in, by all means," turned his head and peered through the steamy gloom. Then he hurriedly looked away again, took the towel off the top of his head and buried his face in it in confusion.

Sumoto *was* technically a hot-spring resort, after all, and there were still a good many inns in such places where the bath was shared by men, women and children. Otani himself had often enough relaxed in such baths not only with Hanae but with other couples, introducing themselves, chatting in a friendly way and thinking nothing of it. It was a good old custom and a pity it was fast dying out.

On the other hand, he couldn't recall ever encountering a member of the staff of an inn in the buff. Still, there always had to be a first time for anything and there was no reason in the world why Mrs. Suekawa shouldn't take a bath in the evening like practically everybody else in Japan. She obviously didn't seem to think there was anything odd about it. He kept his back firmly turned, but he could hear her pull a wooden stool into position on the tiled floor, fill a plastic bowl from one of the several taps placed low along the wall to the left of the bath and splosh its contents over her body, the water gurgling away down one of the drain gratings. He heard her fill it again, heard the towel being dunked and wrung out, the slither and slap of the soapy towel on soft flesh, and then the repeated rinsing.

During the two or three minutes these preliminaries took Mrs. Suekawa kept up a friendly stream of courtesies, to the effect that it had been a beautiful day for the time of the year, that the inspector must be very tired after starting so early, and that she was sorry to have served such a poor breakfast but hoped he would again enjoy his evening meal. Otani did his best to respond with appropriate clichés, while wondering how best to extricate himself from a situation which for all his rationalizing he personally found embarrassing.

Then she was upon him. Almost literally, as one smooth leg was lowered on to the ledge beside him, the second followed and Mrs. Suekawa stepped delicately into the bath. She observed the modest convention of holding her little all-purpose towel in front of her pubic region until it was under water, then draped it over the edge of the bath. Another towel, a dry one, was loosely fastened over her hair. Otherwise, she was as naked as Otani, and smiling at him in the friendliest possible way.

"Ooh, this is the best moment of the day, I always say. Don't you agree?"

"Yes, there's nothing like a bath, is there?" Otani was

70

conscious of the lameness of his reply, but quite pleased to be able to produce one at all in the circumstances, for after lowering herself until the water came up to her chin and remaining in that position for a few seconds she stood up again, facing him from a distance of no more than a yard. She was shorter by an inch or two than Otani and the pressure of the water that reached her armpits lifted and rounded her clearly and attractively visible breasts, while the rest of her body shimmered palely and dimly in the depths. Etsuko Suekawa was probably nearly twenty years older than Craig Kington's blonde pin-up girl, but there was no contest as far as Otani was concerned. Like Hanae who became that tiny bit softer, plumper and more attractive to him with every year that passed, the naked woman standing so near to him was *onnazakari*, in full, mature bloom and with the unmistakable glint of experience and interest in her eye.

"When I was a young girl in Akashi my father owned a sake shop. It was quite successful and we had our own bathroom. Not many families could afford one in those days, and it was lovely to be able to sit in the bath for as long as I liked every night after Father and Mother had finished with it. It was next to the storehouse at the back and the steam used to smell of sake." She smiled in reminiscence. "I really think I used to get a bit tipsy now and then. It was harder to get the wood to heat the water during the war of course . . . and then early in 1945 when I was seventeen the whole place was burned down in an incendiary raid. The one that killed poor Father." She raised her arms gracefully to adjust the towel on her hair and, Otani was certain, to afford him a view of her glistening red nipples as they broke the surface.

"Those were hard times. You were homeless, then?"

"Well, for a short time, but then my mother took a job in a factory in Himeji where they had a dormitory, and I was sent here to Awaji to stay with her cousin and her husband. They were sure by then that Japan was going to be overrun by American soldiers and thought that at my age I'd be safer away from big cities. They took me in, looked after me and arranged my marriage later on, in 1947."

"Really? You have relatives here? In Sumoto?"

"She died a few years ago. He's still alive, though, living not far from here. He's a lawyer, called Tadao Mori."

It was one more thing for Otani's tired mind to assimilate, and he closed his eyes for a second and sighed. The next moment Mrs. Suekawa was sitting beside him on the ledge, massaging the muscles of his neck and shoulders with strong, expert fingers. "You poor man," she murmured. "You must be absolutely exhausted. And you look as if you have a headache. Let me see if I can help."

With part of his mind Otani knew quite well that he was being made a fool of; that she was deliberately pressing her thigh against his and teasingly brushing her breasts against his back. The trouble was that it felt so good, and this wanton woman really did know how to massage. He felt a delicious languor creeping over him and replacing his earlier fatigue, and wanted her to go on for ever.

Then her fingers began to creep slowly lower and the warning bells began to make themselves heard in his mind at last. He realized that within a very short time it would be impossible to sustain even the present flimsy pretense of decorum. The beginnings of a sense of the ridiculous also came to his rescue. He reminded himself that it was at least possible that he was on the point of being seduced by a nude murderess, a situation neither Hercule Poirot nor Nero Wolfe would dream of allowing to arise.

"Thank you so much," he croaked, sliding away from the insistent fingers and half swimming, half creeping to a safe distance. "That was very refreshing."

Etsuko Suekawa sat back on the ledge and directed something between a pout and a knowing smile at him. Her eyelids drooped lazily and she ran the tip of her tongue round her lips before replying. "I'm glad. If you'd like a proper massage before you go to sleep, I'll be happy to give you one in your room."

The only obvious way to get out of the bath was by using the ledge she was sitting on as a step, and as he approached it with his towel now firmly held over his genitals, for one wild moment Otani feared that she would openly embrace him as soon as he was within reach. In fact she obligingly shifted to one side to enable him to climb out, and to his relief kept her back turned while he dried himself off as much as possible, repeatedly wringing out the little towel. When he had reached a state of tacky dampness which he knew from experience was the most that could be hoped for, he thankfully opened the door to the outer dressing area where his yukata was waiting.

"Well, er . . . I'll be off, then," he said feebly, and fled from the sound of splashing.

Chapter 10

"**N**O, NOT REALLY. THE TROUBLE IS THAT SHE REFUSES to discuss it. You know Aki-chan's always been . . . well, self-contained, ever since she was a little girl. But recently she's become so *sullen*." The connection to their house in Rokko wasn't very good but Otani could hear the sadness in Hanae's voice.

"Yes. I've noticed it too. When she isn't spouting Maoism at me. Still, look at it this way, it would be a bit unusual these days to find a university student who *didn't* claim to be a radical, so we must hope it's just a phase, I suppose, and that she doesn't do anything that'll get her into real trouble. Has she put up any new posters in her room? Apart from Che Guevara and that other fellow, I mean? No? Well, that's something."

"Yes, I suppose it is. I went to my cookery class at the Kobe YWCA today and the subject came up. There are several others there with sons or daughters about Aki-chan's age and most of them are just as worried about them as we are. By the way, do you think you might like cassoulet? It's French, a sort of very thick *nabe* with a lot of beans, and pieces of pork, and duck, and spicy sausage. I can get the sausage at the Kobe Delicatessen, I think. And, oh, other things. Very filling.''

"It sounds all right," Otani said dubiously.

"Where are you ringing from, by the way?"

"The bus station. It's pretty well deserted at this time of the evening. Much more private than the phone at the inn.''

"I hope they're taking good care of you there." A vision of the opulently nude Etsuko Suekawa smiling invitingly at him in the bath swam into Otani's mind and he cleared his throat before replying.

"Oh, yes. Fine. I don't much take to the owner, but I must admit he's a good cook. And his wife seems to be going out of her way to . . . well, make me feel at home, oh, and there's a maid who puts me in mind of Akiko. She's a couple of years older, about twenty I'd say. Very left-wing opinions and not a bit shy about airing them. Odd for a girl like that to take a job as a maid in an inn. Anyway, she's good-hearted enough really. She well and truly put me in my place when I first arrived, but now she seems to have decided to try to be helpful. The thing is, she rather fancies the young policeman they've assigned to help me, and he's obviously sweet on her. Odd situation.''

"Perhaps Aki-chan will fall for a policeman. It's a very easy thing to do, as I know from experience.''

"That's a nice thing to say, Ha-chan. I miss you.''

"I miss you too. Did you go out after your supper just so as to phone me?''

"Yes. And to wander about and have a think. It's been a confusing sort of day. I must admit I did take the opportunity to ring a colleague of mine in connection with the case. He's been looking into something for me.''

Hanae knew better than to ask him a direct question about his work. "Well, all I can say is that I hope you'll get it all sorted out and come home soon. Maybe there'll be some news about your next job." They both knew only that it was likely that Otani's stint as head of the prefectural CID would soon be over.

"Ah well, *que sera, sera*." Otani was something of a Doris Day fan and had recently taken to using the phrase from one of her more durable hits. "Where's Akiko now, by the way?" He fed more money into the coin-box. He had chosen one of the red public telephones which accepted hundred-yen as well as ten-yen coins and provided himself with an ample supply of change.

"Out at one of her endless discussion meetings. But I'm sure she'll be back before ten. She may be difficult in some ways but she's a good girl about that."

"Yes. Ha-chan, do you remember that Hiroshige print Father used to like to look at now and then? 'Fox Fire,' I think it was called?"

"Yes, of course. It used to give me the creeps. We still have it of course, in the glory-hole with a lot of his other things. Why do you ask?"

"All those foxes gathered round a tree not far from a village, and some more in the distance. Sort of glowing. I've been trying to remember what the picture was actually supposed to be *about*."

"Fox fire? Well, isn't it the light foxes produce to lure travelers away from the right road? I never did like all those stories about foxes tricking human beings, even the ones that were supposed to be funny. They all had something gruesome about them."

"Luring people away from the right road. That's a thought."

"Are you all right, darling? You sound, well, sort of sad and a bit strange."

"Yes, I'm fine. Just thinking. Foxes can do all manner of things, can't they? Hypnotize men. Disguise themselves as wandering priests, that sort of thing."

"Priests, yes, and woodcutters and so on, but women, mostly. In most of the stories I know a supernatural fox is forever taking the form of a beautiful woman and making some lonely man fall in love with her. Then after a while she usually disappears and it turns out she's stolen all his most precious possessions or turned his savings into grass or something."

"Yes. Thank you for reminding me. Tricky creatures, foxes."

"You really do sound very odd. Are you *sure* you're feeling all right?"

"Mm. A bit tired. And this is a funny sort of place. It'll be nice to be home again but it'll be at least a few days before I'll be able to get away, I expect. Well, I'll say goodnight."

"Know what I suggest?" Hanae's voice was full of anxious concern.

"What?"

"When you get back to the inn, ask them to arrange for an *anma-san* to give you a massage. Those places always have one on call. It'll relax you, make you feel better, and help you to sleep properly. You mustn't overtire yourself, you know."

"Actually, I don't really think—"

"No, I insist. You've made me feel quite worried about you. You go straight back and have that massage. And then you can tell me how much good it did you next time you ring me. Goodnight, darling."

Otani put the phone down and pocketed the unused coins that clattered into the cup at the bottom of the box. He felt warmed and comforted by the conversation with Hanae, though he now rather wished he'd kept off the subject of magical foxes. And her insistence on his having a massage before he went to bed was little short of alarming. It was perfectly true that virtually every inn and hotel in Japan had the phone number of a local masseur who could be summoned within a matter of minutes, and it was commonplace for both male and female guests to book a massage in the privacy of their rooms.

The traditional anma-san was usually a blind, elderly man or woman, highly skilled in locating and working on bunched muscles and aching joints and often able to smooth and soothe away headaches as well as leaving the client in a state of pleasantly drowsy languor. Professional anmas plied an ancient and entirely respectable trade, scrupulously avoiding the forbidden areas of the client's body which was in any case modestly covered by a yukata. They were in no way to be confused with the young women in the abbreviated shorts

77

and skimpy halters who attended the invariably male customers at Turkish baths in the entertainment areas of big cities and offered a variety of sexual services with a tariff of charges.

The trouble was that thanks to Mrs. Suekawa's ministrations in the bath earlier he didn't need a massage, and if he were to order one she would undoubtedly assume that he was accepting her unmistakable offer of her favors and volunteer her own services. He hoped Hanae wouldn't remember to ask him next time if he had followed her instructions. If she did he would simply have to tell her he had, though it probably wouldn't fool her. She had an uncanny ability to see through him when he fibbed to her.

It was a little after nine and the chill of the clear evening contrasted sharply with the mildness of the day. Otani stepped out briskly in the direction of the Tokiwa and then realized that the Inari Shrine was more or less on the way. He was briefly tempted to call on Mrs. Horiuchi, now that he had spoken to the inspector in Akashi and learned that the tailing of her husband had proved to be well worthwhile. The little boy would surely be in bed by nine, after all. Or would he? One never knew these days. And besides, it was hardly proper for a man who knew her husband was away to call on a married woman so late in the evening. No, better to stick to the timetable he had agreed with Higashida and for both of them to go there the following morning.

When he reached the shrine he turned in under the big outer torii anyway, crossed the outer precinct and paused when he reached the stone steps which led to the inner part. By night the soft-drink vending machine and the various signs and exhortations displayed outside the kindergarten building were not so conspicuous, and the whole complex looked less stridently prosperous than it had when Otani had first seen it a little over twelve hours earlier.

He paused before mounting the steps, and at that moment the almost full moon began to rise above the line of trees to his right. Otani had never thought of himself as a particularly superstitious man and considered his nerves to be reasonably robust. Nevertheless he experienced a distinct *frisson* when the sanctuary's two guardian foxes were suddenly illumi-

78

nated by the moonlight. He told himself sternly not to be so foolish. This fox business was becoming ridiculous. The images before him were nothing but lumps of carved stone, presented to the shrine no doubt by some ambitious merchant, social upstart or entrepreneur of a former generation to boost his local reputation. They weren't even particularly well executed, though to be fair the stone must have weathered a good deal over the decades.

Determined not to allow his imagination to run away with him, Otani went up the steps and deliberately examined the pair of fox carvings at close quarters. The bodies and the upright, luxuriant tails were more or less identical, but as usual one of them, the male, was depicted with open mouth and baring his teeth, presumably snarling or whatever foxes do. It was a menacing expression, anyway, and Otani pulled a face at it, finding a curious satisfaction in doing so before crossing to take a close look at its mate.

The female's mouth was closed, the effect altogether more tranquil and demure. The stonemason had done a better job on this one, produced an altogether more . . . he stumbled back, his heart pounding, his body suddenly clammy with sweat in spite of the chill. The damned thing had *smiled* at him. It was impossible, it couldn't be! But it *had* smiled, was *still* smiling at him. Otani shook his head vigorously, blinked several times and rubbed his eyes with fingers that trembled slightly, then pulled out a handkerchief and wiped away the moisture he had produced. Even so his eyes were still swimming and his vision was blurred as he forced himself to look again at the image of the female.

He stood there shivering uncontrollably for a long time, trying by an act of will to banish the lewd, conspiratorial smile from the face of the stone vixen, telling himself over and over again that it was a trick of the moonlight, that he was overtired, that he must simply turn his back and walk away. And all the time he heard Hanae's voice in his mind, repeating the words she had used on the phone . . . ''a supernatural fox is forever taking the form of a beautiful woman and making some lonely man fall in love with her . . . a

79

massage will make you feel better . . . help you to sleep properly . . . I insist . . .''

It was rather late, well after ten, when Otani eventually got back to the Tokiwa. He was more than a little drunk, having finally managed to stumble away from the shrine and find a small bar in a side street where he drank four, or perhaps it was five, glasses of Suntory whisky and water in rapid succession. Fuddled as he was, at least he felt reasonably sane again. As he approached the door of the inn he hoped first that it would be unlocked, next that there would be nobody about so that he could get up to his room without any further encounter with the Suekawa tribe, and lastly that if anyone *was* waiting to see him safely in it would be the oily, servile proprietor or even his crazed old mother. Anybody but Etsuko.

"Okaeri nasai!" she said brightly as soon as he edged his way round the door he had slid only partially open, and that as quietly as possible. "Welcome back! Fancy going out without an overcoat on a cold night like this! You must be frozen.'' She sniffed and then wagged a roguish finger at him. "Aha! Unless I'm much mistaken somebody's had a little something to keep the cold out, and who am I to blame you? My husband goes to his favorite bar every night and never gets back till one or two in the morning.''

Swaying slightly, Otani gazed at her, relieved. She was wearing a simple yukata and her appearance was perfectly wholesome and unthreatening. It had all been pure imagination. She didn't look in the least like the vixen at the shrine, and if she was a murderess he was a . . . well, he was a . . . a magic fox himself. She was just an ordinary, friendly women doing her best to run an inn while tied to a miserable specimen of a man she'd been married off to without any say in the matter. Nice of her to wait up for a guest. Nothing to be ashamed of just because he'd had a few whiskies. Probably quite used to men staggering back a bit the worse for drink.

"Hello,'' he said, managing to kick his shoes off without bending down. He was glad of her help in negotiating the

80

step, but then shook himself free of her arm. "Thank you. Find my own way now. Ready for bed. Been quite a day. G'night."

Etsuko Suekawa followed at a discreet distance and watched him laboriously climb the staircase, quietly humming a catchy little tune she recognized. They were always playing it on the radio. Whatever will be, will be, or something. She thought she'd give him five minutes to get himself to bed, maybe ten. After that, whatever would be, would be.

Chapter 11

IT WAS A NONDESCRIPT SORT OF MORNING, DULL AND GRAY but dry and not particularly cold. Apart from a certain amount of activity in and around the kindergarten the outer precinct was quiet, and their shoes crunched loudly on the gravel as Otani set a brisk pace toward the steps. When the two men were about five yards short of the fox images he stopped in his tracks and stared long and hard at them. Then he nodded his head once and moved on.

"If I might be permitted to ask, sir, is there any word from Akashi?" Desperate to establish some sort of communication, Higashida almost blurted the words out as they trudged up the steps to the inner sanctuary. Otani had scarcely uttered a word since arriving early at headquarters. After the gruffest of good mornings he had closeted himself in his temporary office for about twenty minutes with the material they had taken from Craig Kington's room. Then, carrying a small furoshiki-wrapped bundle, he had left the building again as abruptly as he had entered it, beckoning the patiently waiting Higashida to follow him.

"Yes. I spoke to the inspector there yesterday evening. You'll find out the details when we talk to the priest later today. I'll want him met by a couple of uniformed men at the Iwaya car ferry terminal this afternoon, by the way. Or evening. Akashi will be letting us know which one he takes. He's to be escorted directly to headquarters here, so that we can talk to him before he's spoken to his wife. If they don't have a car available at the Iwaya police station one will have to be sent from here. Horiuchi can be allowed to drive his own car, of course. Can you arrange that?''

"Yes, sir. Of course. You mean he's to be arrested, sir?'' He sounded enthusiastic about the prospect.

"No. Just invited to cooperate with us in our inquiries. By the way, sorry if I was a bit short with you earlier.''

"Oh, not at all, sir. You are, er, feeling quite well?''

"I had a rather disturbed night. There's some wretched dog that has a habit of barking in the middle of the night near the inn. I'm all right now though, thanks, apart from a bit of a headache.'' They were nearing the enclosure in which the priest's house stood, and on cue the dog chained outside set up a furious clamor.

"It couldn't be this one, sir?'' Higashida had to bellow to make himself heard over the racket. "It makes enough row.''

"NO. DIFFERENT SOUnd entirely . . .'' Otani's fortissimo reply became a rapid diminuendo as Mrs. Horiuchi opened the house door and once more silenced the dog with an inaudible word. They walked up the path and bowed politely.

"Good morning, gentlemen. Do please come in.''

"Good morning, madam.'' Otani had forgotten what a delightful speaking voice she had. "You have, I believe, met Officer Higashida before.''

"Very briefly, a few days ago. Good morning, officer.''

Naomi Horiuchi backed into the house to allow them to enter. She had clearly prepared herself for the interview. She was carefully, even excessively made up for nine in the morning, her hair was perfectly arranged and she was wearing a rich blue dress of soft wool that even to Otani's untutored eye looked expensive.

The interior of the house looked expensive too. It was in the traditional style, and the finest authentic materials seemed to have been used rather than the much cheaper plastic veneers and substitutes so common in newly constructed houses. Only costly *hinoki* timber had that marvelous soft, honey-colored glow about it, that uniquely silky finish, and only one slender cypress trunk in twenty when stripped of its bark and lovingly, patiently polished by hand could become such an exquisite feature of a living-room alcove.

The Horiuchi residence even smelt expensive. The fragrance was that of new, best-quality tatami matting, austerely pure and deeply satisfying. Otani loved it. The fact that in the morning light the stone foxes could be seen clearly as the commonplace objects they were, with nothing in the least special about the head of the female, had indeed done much to lighten his grim mood. The smell of the fresh tatami helped even more to calm him and put him in the right frame of mind to approach the difficult task he faced.

"You have a beautiful house, madam," he said with complete sincerity when Naomi Horiuchi returned, having excused herself after settling them on silk brocade zabuton cushions at a brilliantly polished black lacquer table. She brought green tea and small bean-jam cakes individually wrapped in soft rice-paper, and joined them at the table. "It can't be easy to keep it looking so elegant with an eight-year-old boy on the premises."

She smiled calmly. "Thank you, but it's a very ordinary house and I can assure you that my son's room doesn't look in the least like this one. He isn't allowed in here on his own, I might add, and very seldom even when we have guests."

"It must feel rather strange living in the middle of a fair-sized town but nevertheless in such an isolated situation, with no neighbors. Is that why you keep a dog?"

"Oh, I should have apologized earlier for Hachiko. My husband gave him that name, after the famous one. You know, the one they put up a statue to in front of Shibuya Station in Tokyo. I'm sorry he's so noisy when anybody he doesn't know comes near the house."

"Hachiko because he's as faithful as his namesake?"

"Hardly." Her giggle was as attractive as her speaking voice. "To answer your questions, no, not really. This is a very busy shrine, especially at weekends and holidays, and

84

I sometimes wish we had a bit more privacy, not less. All the same, it is very quiet at night, though, and since my husband has to be away quite often we acquired Hachiko mainly as a guard dog. He also discourages people visiting the shrine from straying on to our private property.''

"I see.'' It was time to begin to get to the point, and Otani cleared his throat. "Mrs. Horiuchi, when we spoke briefly yesterday morning I explained that I should be grateful if you would provide us with a formal statement, and you kindly agreed to this.''

She inclined her head. "By all means.''

"Thank you. Now what I should like to do is go over the ground first in a preliminary way, after which we'll draw up a draft summary of your replies in the proper form and submit it to you. Needless to say you'll only put your seal to it if you are satisfied that it's accurate.''

"I understand.''

"Fine. Then let me begin at the beginning. When did you first become aware of the fact that something untoward had happened in the inner shrine precinct?''

"When I was seeing my son off to school that morning.'' She looked at Higashida, who was busily taking notes. "This officer came up to us and barred the way, mentioning something about an accident. I explained that accident or no accident my son had to go to school, and he very kindly offered to see him safely out of the grounds.''

"And then you came back into the house?''

"Yes. My husband was getting ready to go over to the sanctuary as usual and I helped him to put on his robes.''

"No doubt you mentioned to him what Officer Higashida had said to you?''

"I did, yes, but he's always in a serious, rather preoccupied frame of mind when he's about to conduct the morning rituals and it's quite possible he didn't even hear what I said.''

"Now, when did you discover the true nature of what this officer had very properly at that stage referred to as an accident?''

"Not until about lunchtime, when the head teacher at the kindergarten came and told me there'd been a murder. She'd seen the ambulance, and police coming and going, and found out all about it.''

''*All* about it? Including the identity of the victim?''

''No. I didn't find that out until later.''

''Who told you?''

Her hesitation before she replied was so slight as to be barely noticeable, but Otani's antennae were sensitive enough to register it. ''I really can't remember. I must admit that after she left—the kindergarten head, I mean—I spent quite a while on the phone ringing various friends and acquaintances and heard all sorts of bits and pieces of gossip. The news seemed to be all over town by then, and two or three people said it was one of the foreign teachers. As I say, I can't recall who first mentioned the name.''

''The name of Craig Kington?''

''Yes.''

''Mrs. Horiuchi, forgive me for speaking very frankly, but if I may say so you don't seem very upset by all this business.''

''Should I be?''

''That's not for me to say. But let me put it this way. I don't know a great deal about Shinto but I imagine that your husband for his part took a very serious view of the matter when he learned that a man had been killed within the precincts, and so close to the sanctuary at that.''

''No doubt he'll tell you so himself when he gets back, but he did, yes. He explained to me afterward that he'd had to conduct special, very elaborate purification ceremonies. They took him ages, I believe.''

''No doubt. But apart from being interested enough to ring up a few friends and discuss it after you heard the news, you weren't particularly bothered personally by the fact that murder had been done so near your house?''

''Well, it's not a very nice thing to happen, is it? That goes without saying. But I don't really see what it had or has to do with me personally.''

''Ah. Let me ask a different question altogether, then. Have you any idea at all who might have killed Craig Kington?''

86

"Not the remotest. Apart from the fact that he'd been living here in Sumoto for a few months with the other American, I never knew a thing about the man."

Otani scratched his head in ostentatious puzzlement. "But he gave you English conversation lessons, didn't he?"

"Me? English conversation? What an extraordinary thing to say! Who on earth told you that?"

"His colleague, Mr. Wilson. Isn't that so, Officer Higashida?"

"Yes, sir. That is to say, Mrs. Horiuchi's name is on the list of Mr. Kington's pupils he provided."

Naomi Horiuchi looked at Higashida as though he were something offensive the cat had brought in, and was hardly less haughty when she turned back to Otani.

"I've never heard of anything so ridiculous in my life. There must be some mistake. Some other Horiuchi, possibly. It is not that uncommon a name."

"I do apologize if there has been a slip-up. We'll check again. Well, I think that's all for the moment and I do thank you for your help. As I said earlier, we'll prepare a draft statement and have somebody bring it here and leave it with you to look at. Perhaps in the meantime you wouldn't mind just jotting down the names of the friends you rang that morning, and try to recall which one it was who first mentioned Craig Kington's name."

Otani placed both hands flat on the table to lever himself up, then hastily removed them and looked with consternation at the palm-prints he had left on the glossy lacquer. "Oh, dear. Clumsy of me." He took out his handkerchief and gently polished the marks away. "You're still expecting your husband back this afternoon or this evening? He hasn't rung by any chance to let you know which?"

"No, and I'd be astonished if he were ever to do such a thing."

"Ah. Well, he's a very busy man, I'm sure. Even so, perhaps he'll be able to spare us a few minutes tomorrow. Anyway, we must be off now." Otani deliberately made a great to-do about getting up, not completely confident that Higashida would be able to prevent his inside knowledge from showing in his face. Then as Naomi Horiuchi went ahead to open the door to the entrance hall he hung back and spoke in a timid little voice.

"Excuse me, but may I ask a great personal favor?"

It was obvious that she was now anxious to be rid of them, but probably assuming that he wanted to use the lavatory she nodded politely. "Of course."

Otani fiddled with the knot securing the little bundle he had kept beside him throughout. "It's just that this is one of the most handsome rooms I've ever seen in a private house. I wonder if you'd allow me to take a photo of it?"

"Oh. I suppose so, if you want to."

"How kind. It won't take a moment. I've got one of these Polaroid cameras, you see. Instant prints." He showed her the camera he had brought. "The quality's surprisingly good and it has all the usual features of a conventional camera, ten-second delay so that you can take your own picture, and so forth."

"Well, it took all her self-control to get us out of there without going into hysterics," Otani said with satisfaction as he went out of the gate Higashida was holding open for him. "I congratulate you on your deadpan face at the end, by the way. Quickly, now, round the corner to the shrine office. I hope there's nobody there yet."

They were in luck. Higashida stood by bemused while Otani looked round furtively and then, satisfied that the coast was clear, took a small pair of pliers from his pocket. "Give me a leg up, will you? Come *on*, Higashida-kun!" He almost dragged him to the corner of the small wooden building, and pointed to its roof, where two telephone wires joined a ceramic holder. Belatedly grasping what was needed of him, Higashida seized Otani round the knees and hoisted him high enough for him to reach and deftly sever both wires.

Back on the ground, Otani looked at him gravely. "Aiding and abetting willful damage to the property of the National Telephone and Telegraph Corporation, that was. Good reason for you to keep all this under your hat. Now let's get out of here and I'll explain on the way. Cutting those wires won't hold her back all that long, she hasn't got far to go to find a payphone, but it will give her that little bit more to think about. And of course it'll be a few hours at least before it's repaired and that should make it pretty well impossible for the priest to get in touch with her before we have our little chat with him.''

"Sorry, sir, I'm not with you."

"Hardly your fault. I had information you didn't. She's lying, and now she's sitting there realizing she was very fool-ish indeed to deny she was a pupil of Kington's when we know perfectly well she was. I cut the phone because my guess is that she'll now go to some lengths to arrange for two or three close friends to perjure themselves by saying she did ring them that morning."

"But why all that business about the photograph? It was certainly all she could do to keep a grip on herself while you were taking it."

"It was the camera that worried her." Otani pulled the picture he had taken out of his jacket pocket and looked at it. It didn't do justice to the beauty of the room, but was clear enough. "The camera was in one of the drawers of Kington's desk. You didn't see me put it in the holdall with the other stuff. She recognized it the moment she saw it, or thought it was an identical model I'd brought along to trap her. Here, hold the picture a minute."

He gave it to Higashida and then took from his wallet the one Kington had been carrying when he was killed. He held it blank side uppermost and looked sideways at Higashida. "I'm not at all sure I ought to let you see this," he said. "But I think I will, provided you give me your word you won't mention it to a living soul or refer to it in any note or report."

"Of course not, sir."

Otani still hesitated. "Think carefully. I don't want to land you in any sort of trouble. I'm skating round the regulations at the moment and I won't think any the worse of you if you'd prefer not to be associated with anything irregular. I do have what I think are very good reasons for keeping this strictly confidential for the time being, and I'm quite prepared to see this through on my own."

"You can trust me, sir. I'd be proud to help."

"Thank you. And I'd be grateful for your help." He handed over the second Polaroid print and watched the young man's face as he looked at it. "Recognize the room?"

"Yes, sir." His voice sounded strangulated, but intelligible.

"Recognize the people?"

"Yes, sir."

"Of course you do. Right, give them back, and let's be on our way. By the way," Otani went on in a conversational tone as they moved on, "about the little ceramic fox that was found on the body. The old chap who was first on the scene swore he never touched it?"

"Absolutely, sir."

"And you dusted it for prints yourself?"

"Yes. We have basic gear at headquarters. And it was easy to match the prints against the one the town office has on record for Kington. The same as the one in his alien registration card, of course."

"And then you put it in that plastic bag yourself, right? And stowed it in a locker with his clothes and the things in the envelope?"

"That's right, sir."

Otani nodded thoughtfully, and remained silent until they arrived back at headquarters.

Chapter 12

THE TAP ON HIS DOOR WAS SO HESITANT THAT OTANI wasn't sure he had heard it. Head raised, he waited until it was repeated, and then called out an invitation to whoever it was to come in. It proved to be Inspector Takada, who opened the door a foot or so and peeped round it at him. Otani stood up in deference to the senior man who was still seemingly reluctant to enter.

"Ah, Inspector! Good morning to you. Do please come in."

"Good morning. I do so hesitate to intrude, but perhaps just for a moment . . ."

On the day of Otani's arrival in Sumoto Takada had been wearing uniform, but now he was dressed in a dark blue suit complete with waistcoat, so roomily cut that it made him look even bulkier than he was. His shirt was one of the old-fashioned kind, striped but with a separate stiff white collar, and his tie was also blue, with a gold-colored cogwheel device embroidered on it just above the V of the waistcoat. Otani recognized it, and the matching little cogwheel badge in his lapel. There was a spare chair for a visitor but Takada drifted over to the window and stared out of it, so Otani felt

91

obliged to remain on his feet. Several seconds passed before Otani spoke to his back.

"I see you're a Rotarian, Inspector."

Takada turned to face him, a brief but infinitely satisfied smile flickering across his face. "Yes, I have that honor," he said. "You recognize the insignia." His eyes widened. "You are not by any chance also . . . ?"

"Dear me, no, I'm not nearly important enough. I do have one or two Rotarian acquaintances." Otani thought it tactful not to add that one of them was currently lobbying hard to get him elected to the prestigious Kobe South Rotary Club. Only the Baron might just manage to rally enough influential supporters, and the outcome was by no means certain.

Everybody still called Maeda-san "the Baron," though he had, like all the other members of the former House of Peers, lost his title in 1946. He had more than made up for it by prospering mightily as a wily businessman, and was indeed currently the chairman of the Kobe Chamber of Commerce as well as a power in the national federation of economic organizations. In spite of all this he still found time to watch over the Otanis. As a captain in the Imperial Navy the Baron had been his commanding officer during the eighteen-year-old Otani's few months of service as a junior lieutenant in naval intelligence; and he and his late wife had brought the Otanis together and acted as the go-betweens for their marriage. It occurred to Otani while Takada took his time over replying that as matters stood in Sumoto he could do with a word or two of advice from the Baron.

"Well, perhaps it's rather unseemly for me to be the one to say it," Takada said, still smug, "but over the years I do seem to have become accepted as one of Sumoto's more prominent citizens."

"That goes without saying, I'm sure. Won't you sit down, Inspector? I feel a little guilty, actually. I realize I should have submitted a progress report to you, but I know you're very busy and—"

"Oh, how right you are! What with the responsibilities of the post here and the demands made on its occupant, I sometimes wonder how one manages to keep one's head above water. And on top of everything else, today is the weekly luncheon meeting of the Sumoto Rotarians. It's one I dare not miss, you see.'' He sighed. ''There's so much on hand that there's little prospect of my being able to 'make up' at any other club within the next week. The thing is, our club is very strongly placed to claim the quarterly attendance record for the Kansai region. But I'm running on, running on. Thank you, but no, I won't sit down. And my dear Inspector, there is absolutely no call for a progress report, as you put it. I'm sure you're doing a splendid job.''

''Well, it's good of you to say so. I hope to be able to justify your confidence in me, and it's made things a lot easier to have been given such a free hand. Not to mention the services of Patrolman Higashida as an assistant. He strikes me as being an exceptionally promising young man.''

''A free hand, yes, absolutely. It isn't for an amateur like me to get in the way of the expert. And indeed I only looked in now just to . . . well, ordinarily I wouldn't dream of—''

''Is something troubling you, Inspector?'' Otani gazed at Takada equably. It was obvious that something was, and Otani considered that it was high time the older man came out with it.

''Oh, hardly *troubling*, you know. No, that would be putting it altogether too strongly.''

''But there is something you feel you should mention?''

''Well—I must say it does help, I mean your proving to be so well informed about Rotary—you'll understand, I know, that it's imperative for a man in my position to have due regard to the sensitivities of my fellow Rotarians, and . . .''

''Of course. And . . . ?''

''And, well, frankly speaking I'm bound to say that I was just a trifle concerned to learn that you had—'' Takada turned away again and mumbled the next words at the window— ''given instructions for Horiuchi-sensei to be met at the Iwaya ferry terminal later today.''

''That's correct, yes. I hadn't realized he's a Rotarian too.''

''No reason why you should have known,'' Takada said in the manner of one doing his best to be fair-minded as he swung back to face Otani. ''Still, all's well that ends well.''

His smile of relief faded when he registered the expression on Otani's face.

"I'm afraid I wasn't entirely clear in my own mind to what extent you'd authorized me to call on executive support beyond what Higashida can do personally. I'm sorry. Perhaps I should have sent him to Iwaya instead of asking him to arrange things from this end. Certainly in the circumstances I was remiss in not clearing it with you."

"Well, perhaps, but it's rather academic now, isn't it? Water under the bridge. As I say, you couldn't have known that the priest would have been greatly offended had he—"

"Inspector Takada." Otani interjected the words very quietly, but Takada closed his mouth at once. "Am I to infer from what you have just said that you have countermanded the arrangements made for Horiuchi to be escorted here for questioning direct from the ferry?"

"Why yes, of course. As I have explained and I am sure you now accept, such a course of action is self-evidently out of the question in the case of a prominent person such as Horiuchi-sensei, who will however, I am sure, be quite agreeable to—"

"I see."

"Yes. I . . . I was sure you would." After a silence that dragged on painfully but which Otani had no intention of being the first to break, Takada made an awkward little noise in the back of his throat and headed for the door. "Well, then, I must be on my way. Must record my attendance before the bell goes, you know."

"Just one question if I may, Inspector."

"Yes. Of course, what is it?"

"It's just possible that—oh, never mind. I mustn't keep you from your meeting."

Higashida took up his position in front of the Mazda and Otani rapped on the driver's window. The man at the wheel frowned at him, hesitated and then wound the window down a bare inch or so.

"Excuse me. Is your name Chiaki Horiuchi? Are you the priest in charge of the Inari Shrine in Sumoto?"

"My name's Horiuchi, yes. What do you want?"

Otani showed him his warrant card. "Otani, Tetsuo. Inspector, criminal investigation, Hyogo prefectural police. Go forward about twenty meters, please, and pull in over there so you aren't blocking the cars behind you." He moved away toward the point he had indicated, beckoning Higashida to follow. While their backs were turned Otani half expected Horiuchi to make a break for it and wondered what should be done if he did. Judging from the peremptory sounding of two, maybe three car horns by drivers he was holding up, Horiuchi took his time over deciding to do what he had been told. Do it he did, though, and when he had parked the car he opened the door and got out.

Having caught no more than a glimpse of him as he had driven out of the Inari Shrine at speed the previous morning, Otani subjected the priest to a leisurely scrutiny. Chiaki Horiuchi was, he guessed, around forty: six or seven years older than his wife. He was not particularly tall but was thick-set and looked fit, and Otani thought his fleshy face with its beetle brows and fierce, hot-looking eyes would probably look quite impressive above his priestly robes. On this occasion, however, he was wearing an expensive-looking but rather flashily cut gray chalk-striped suit with a tie which was no more restful to the eye; in fact he looked a bit of a thug.

"Well, what is it?" he demanded. "I'm a busy man."

"Successful trip?" Otani inquired politely, still ostentatiously looking him over.

"I don't see what that's got to do with you. What is all this?"

"Come now, Horiuchi-san." Having deliberately used the everyday form of address rather than using the honorific title *sensei* his status entitled him to, Otani expected the priest to bristle, and as Otani continued he did. "You are well aware that a man was murdered in the inner precinct of the Inari Shrine in Sumoto a few days ago. You must have been expecting to be asked to assist the police in the investigation."

Horiuchi's unpleasing scowl grew even more hostile. "I'm aware that a man's body was found, but I know nothing whatever about the circumstances, needless to say. A man of your

95

seniority ought to have realized I'd have been perfectly willing to talk to you if you'd approached me in a civilized way. As it is, I shall have a thing or two to say to Inspector Takada about your behavior in waylaying me like this. What are you doing here at Iwaya anyway? How did you know I was on this ferry?"

"You weren't expecting us? Your wife wasn't sure, but she thought you'd get back to Iwaya either now or this evening, so we hoped for the best. As a matter of fact this officer and I did have a bit of a problem over transport, so in the end we came by taxi. Anyway, here we are and here you are, and I have a few questions to put to you. If you're agreeable we could sit and talk in your car, or we could go and have a cup of coffee somewhere if you'd prefer that. Won't keep you long."

Horiuchi thrust his face close to Otani's. "Let me tell you something, Inspector Whoever-you-are, you aren't going to keep me at all. I'm going home, and if the Sumoto police have business with me Inspector Takada can ring up and make an appointment."

Otani shook his head sorrowfully. "I really think it would be better if you were to cooperate, you know. You see, it's prefectural police headquarters in Kobe I'm acting for, not the Sumoto police. And I'm not sure your business associates in Kobe would be too pleased to hear you'd been seen calling on them during the past twenty-four hours with this mess hanging over your head. What do you think?"

"Kobe? Business associates? What are you driving at?"

"I think you know. My colleagues there tell me they have some nice pictures, including one of you being seen off by quite a senior man in the Yamamoto outfit. But there's no need for him to be bothered if you'll just be reasonable. So, no more bluster. It might be effective with Inspector Takada but I assure you it doesn't work with me. Shall we get in the car? I'd like to tell you about the chat we had with your wife in your delightful house this morning."

Chapter 13

"**W**E'LL GO BACK BY BUS," OTANI SAID AS THEY watched Horiuchi drive off in a foul temper some forty minutes later. "The way he drives, we'd never get to Sumoto before him even if we went by taxi. And we can talk on the bus."

"Do you think he will lodge a complaint with Inspector Takada, sir?"

Otani shook his head slowly. "I very much doubt it. You can bet the inspector will find out we shanghaied Horiuchi after all—and not necessarily from me—but our friend will probably think twice about doing anything silly. Sillier than he has already, I mean." They ambled toward the uncovered turnaround where two buses were standing, one of them bound for Sumoto and according to the timetable due to depart in eight minutes. Some passengers were already on board but there were plenty of double seats free and Otani chose one near the back.

"Even if Horiuchi does make a fuss you need have no anxiety about your own position so far as this afternoon's work is concerned, by the way. It's true that the inspector tried to dissuade me from intercepting him, but you've simply been following instructions. I shall be explaining all my actions to the prefectural commander when I get back to Kobe.'' He smiled to himself. ''If only to make sure I can claim a refund on our taxi fare. And there'll be no black mark against your name, I can assure you.''

''Yes, sir. Thank you, sir.''

''You sound a bit dubious. Let me put it another way, strictly between ourselves. As you know, Inspector Takada is due to retire in a few months anyway. Well, for various reasons I have a feeling the effective date might be brought forward, but that's by the way. There are more important things to discuss. Horiuchi, mainly. You've seen him before, of course, all done up in his robes. What did you make of him off duty, as it were? Your frank opinion.''

''Sir, I think he's an objectionable man.''

''What, because he doesn't like foreigners? I find them pretty hard to cope with myself.''

''No, I don't mean just that. There's something about him that made my flesh creep more and more as he went on. At first he was so rattled by what you said about his business in Kobe—''

''I'm sorry I can't enlighten you properly about that just yet, Higashida. But you can take it from me that for a priest he has some unexpected friends. Go on.''

''Yes, sir. Well, he was obviously watching his tongue very carefully at first after he decided he'd better answer your questions after all. And if he'd just stuck to his line it would have been difficult to prove he was lying.''

''You mean all that stuff about being in a kind of trance when he was on his way to recite his daily rigmarole in the sanctuary?'' Higashida looked slightly shocked by Otani's irreverence.

''Well, yes. I mean, for all we know Shinto priests might genuinely be in a funny state of mind then. It's at least possible that he wasn't listening when his wife told him what had happened when she was getting the boy off to school. And that he didn't take in what was happening when he passed by.''

''Just barely possible, perhaps, but if it came to the point he might have a job persuading the district prosecutor in

Kobe to believe it. Ah, we're off. Good. Still, he was a bit more forthcoming later, wasn't he?'' They had been keeping their voices low, but the rumble of the engine as the bus lurched into motion and headed south down the coast road enabled them to revert to a normal conversational tone without much chance of being overheard.

"He certainly was. Once you got him on to the subject of foreigners. I mean, it isn't just a matter of not liking them. He was practically raving.''

"We're a funny people, you know, Higashida. If you look at Japanese history over the past hundred years you'll see that we swing from extreme to extreme, either besotted with or detesting everything foreign. And not only the last hundred years, come to that. There's nothing special about Horiuchi. He's just an old-fashioned gaijin-hating right-winger. There were plenty like him before and during the war; then everybody suddenly became peace-loving, democratic and pro-Western. For the time being he's one of a small but noisy minority. But you know, in spite of all the rumpus people like your friend Noriko Ito and my daughter create, I've noticed a trend back to the old ideas in the past few years. I rather fancy the Tokyo Olympics triggered it off. People began to feel proud of being Japanese again and didn't mind saying so. You never know, Horiuchi's ideas might come back into fashion one of these days. At least you know where you are with him. He hates all foreigners on principle, and Christian missionaries in particular.''

"He said he'd never set eyes on either of the two Americans, sir.''

"I expect to know before long whether or not he's lying. I think he is. But either way it doesn't affect my argument. Those two young gaijin have certainly made an impact during the few months they've been living in Sumoto. They must have stuck out like a sore thumb from day one, and been the subject of endless gossip. Worse than hippies, really, because they look respectable. Yet there they were in an otherwise one hundred percent Japanese town preaching an alien, American brand of Christianity. The awareness of their presence alone must have outraged Horiuchi. Three hundred years ago the Japanese authorities used to kill Christians, you know. Not only foreign missionaries, the Japanese they converted too. Horiuchi probably thinks of those as the good old days.''

"All the same, sir, I got the impression that he doesn't know about his wife and Kington . . . do you think his anti-foreign feelings are strong enough for him to have killed the American anyway?'' Otani looked out of the window for a while before replying.

"I don't know. Given his general attitudes, discovering that his wife was on, shall we say, friendly terms with a foreign missionary would be quite enough to tip him over the brink. But I'm rather inclined to agree with you. He got so excited that I think he would have let something slip if he does know.''

"And in any case if he did he'd probably kill her too, wouldn't he? And Mrs. Horiuchi's reaction to that camera suggests that he doesn't know and she's terrified of the idea that he might find out.''

"Quite right. You're thinking like a detective.'' Otani looked out of the window again to give Higashida time to digest the compliment. Then he sighed and turned back to him. "Horiuchi is clearly a suspect. I just wish there weren't quite so many others, don't you?''

"Surely there aren't that many, sir?''

"Count them for yourself, Higashida. Remember the necessary qualifications: motive, means, opportunity. We've just been discussing one possible motive: religious or political prejudice. And that alone puts Horiuchi on our list. Anybody else?''

Higashida pondered but soon shook his head.

"No? Well, fair enough from your point of view I suppose, because you were upstairs when Gary Wilson was pouring out his heart to me. He's convinced that Kington had betrayed their religion—whatever it is—and said he was glad Kington was dead. So Wilson's on the list too, and like Horiuchi he could additionally have been motivated by jealousy. It's pretty clear that Kington not only chased women but was good at catching them too, and there's no point in your looking at me like that, Higashida. Like Horiuchi, Wilson is obviously a fanatic consumed by anger and hatred, and in his case I'd say he was as deeply jealous about Kington's success with women as he'd be horrified to admit even to himself."

"Yes. I see what you're driving at, sir. And of course both the priest and the American could easily have made an opportunity to kill him."

"Quite. And I think we can take it for granted that absolutely anybody could have got hold of a sharp knife and actually stabbed Kington in the darkness. Except old Mrs. Suekawa. I think we have to rule her out on grounds of physical incapacity. She's just too old and frail. What are you grinning at, may I ask?"

"Sorry, sir. It's just that . . . well, you haven't seriously considered the old woman as a possible suspect, have you?"

"Certainly I have, Patrolman. Old Mrs. Suekawa, her son, and his wife. Cast your mind back two or three days, if it really is only that long ago. I feel as if I've been here for months. It was you who booked me in at the Tokiwa in the first place, remember, partly because you thought the people there might know something about the murder. You should feel complimented when I say that I now think it quite possible one of them committed it."

"I thought they might know something, but it never entered my head that any of them might have actually done it. So you reckon there are five, well, call it four and a half suspects, sir? Horiuchi, Wilson, the Suekawas and the old lady?"

"More. There's also Mrs. Horiuchi, and Tadao Mori who turns out to be Mrs. Suekawa's uncle or cousin or something by marriage. And, unlikely I admit but just possible and you might as well face it, Noriko Ito."

"But surely none of those have a motive?"

"Come now, you must be half asleep! Mrs. Horiuchi most certainly has a motive. A complex of motives, indeed. Kington might have been blackmailing her, she might have been jealous of one or more of his other women, she might simply have panicked at the idea of her husband finding out. Now take Etsuko Suekawa. She also knew Kington, how well we can't say." Otani cleared his throat which had become unaccountably dry. "So she could have somewhat similar motives to Naomi Horiuchi's. And her husband could have suspected and become murderously jealous, possibly egged on by the old woman. Noriko Ito could have had a political motive: maybe Kington had been playing rather too effective a role in their discussion meetings and had begun to undermine the revolutionary convictions of the comrades."

"You don't really mean that, sir," Higashida said stiffly, and Otani darted a sidelong look at him.

"No, you're quite right, I don't. In fact Miss Ito's not really a suspect at all. It's probably rash of me, but I think of her as an ally, actually."

Higashida beamed at him, greatly encouraged. "That still leaves Mori, sir. What reason could he possibly have for wanting to get rid of Kington?"

Otani flapped a hand wearily. "Give me time and I'll think of one. I'm working on it." He was conscious of being very tired, and closed his eyes for a moment.

The next thing of which he became aware was a strong young hand gripping his wrist and shaking his forearm, and a voice in his ear. "We're almost there, sir. Next stop." Half asleep, Otani stumbled off the bus after Higashida, letting him pay their fares. Then, slightly revived by being on his feet again in the cool air of early evening, he told Higashida to call for him at the Tokiwa at eight-thirty the next morning and bade him goodnight.

"Yes, yes, I know where I am. I'll enjoy the short stroll to the inn. What's the time? Just after six? Quite enough for one day I think. Off you go. Goodnight."

Otani dawdled along, glad to be on his own again, and surprised at himself for having been so frank with the young assistant he had known for so short a time. At least he'd had the sense to keep quiet about the remaining two possibilities. It was a serious breach of etiquette on his part to have allowed himself to be openly critical of Inspector Takada in conversation with one of his most junior staff, but it would have been far worse to let Higashida know that as of that morning Takada had joined the list of suspects. And of course it was out of the question to admit that the more he thought about Tadao Mori's absurd theory that Kington had been killed by a fox-spirit the more he was persuaded that Mori might conceivably be right.

Meantime there were who knew what hazards lying in wait for him at the inn. Otani squared his shoulders and stepped out more briskly. One thing was certain. For all he cared the entire chorus of the Takarazuka All-Girl Revue Company could share the bath with him. If they did, he would ignore them. And come what may, he would retire to bed immediately after he had eaten his evening meal.

Alone.

Chapter 14

OTANI REALIZED THAT SOMETHING UNTOWARD WAS afoot at the Tokiwa almost as soon as he awakened from the best night's sleep he had known for some time and peered at his watch to discover that it was already after seven-thirty. As he flapped along the corridor in his yukata and slippers toward the lavatory and wash-place at the end he heard a series of bumps on the floor below as though items of heavy furniture were being shoved about with unnecessary violence, the sound of Suekawa's voice raised in anger, and for one blood-chilling moment what sounded like a scream, a scream suppressed almost at once.

Otani hurried to the head of the stairs but by the time he got there the voices he could hear—one male and two, no, three female—sounded a little more controlled. He wondered briefly whether to go down as he was and find out what was going on, but then decided to get dressed first. His morning shave could wait, but he quickly washed his face and hands, returned to his room and began to scramble into his clothes. He was fastening his trousers when he heard Noriko announce herself outside before sliding the door open and entering carrying a tray. She was in what Otani was coming to think of as her normal clothes: jeans and a sweater, but this time one which more or less fitted her and was worn over a blouse or shirt of some kind. She looked pale and her lips were compressed.

"Good morning, Miss Ito."

"Morning. Afraid you can only have coffee for the moment. It's chaos down there."

"What's been going on? It sounded like the end of the world a few minutes ago."

"A few *minutes*? Are you on sleeping pills or something? I should have thought the rumpus going on when I got here just before seven would have been enough to wake the dead, and from what they were shouting at each other I got the impression that the three of them have been at it half the night."

"At *what*, exactly? A family quarrel?"

"What else? That lot make me sick."

"The old woman's fox again?"

"That and other things. But don't worry, I don't think it's a case for the police except that you're having to go without breakfast. Drink your coffee anyway."

"Bother breakfast, it isn't a patch on supper anyway." All the same, Otani swallowed a mouthful of coffee and felt better for it. "May I ask you a couple of questions? Personal questions?"

"If they have anything to do with what might or might not have happened between me and Craig Kington, no."

"Nothing like that. No, the first one is this. What on earth is a person like you doing here working as a maid?"

"It's a perfectly honorable job. You said your own daughter's a part-time waitress. Not much difference."

"I never suggested for a second it isn't an honorable job. You're simply evading the question, but I can't make you answer."

"Why are you so keen to know?"

"Lots of reasons. You obviously can't stand Suekawa, you're upset by their rows, you have to work demanding hours and frankly I'd be surprised if the pay's that good. A person like you could easily get a much more interesting job . . . you might have to go to Kobe to find a really good one,

105

but—'' He just stopped short of asking her whether she'd ever thought about a career in the police force.

"Sorry, you'll just have to wonder. Let's just say personal reasons. You're welcome to try me with your other question if you like.''

"All right, but I have to confide in you before I ask it. Look, when I went to see that fellow Mori and he came out with all this business about the Suekawas being a fox-possessing family I thought he wasn't quite all there and that it was a lot of tomfoolery. But I'll be quite frank with you, some very odd things have been happening to me while I've been here. In the middle of the first night—before I even met Mori—I heard this weird noise, but assumed it was a dog somewhere in the neighborhood. On the other hand it wasn't like any normal barking . . . well, I see I need not spell out what I was going to say. Then when I was at the Inari Shrine the other evening I had a very disturbing hallucination of some kind, and . . . well, there have been one or two other strange experiences. Anyway, the upshot is that I've come around to the idea that Mori might be perfectly sane, and honestly believe in some sort of occult influence which for purposes of discussion we might as well call fox-possession. And I'm quite willing to take it on trust that the old lady is convinced she's got a spirit fox, and that she can keep it on her side by putting out tofu for it every night. Right, now this is my question. Do you?''

"Do I believe in fox-spirits? Obviously not. I believe in dialectical materialism.''

"So you do. No, I'm not being patronizing, I assure you. All right, but when I first mentioned Mori's theory to you, I remember you reacted with a certain amount of amusement. You obviously knew all about old Mrs. Suekawa's fox. Is there quite a bit of talk about it in the neighborhood, would you say?''

"A certain amount, but it's one of those silly things. Younger people pay no attention or treat it as a joke. There may be one or two about her own age who take it seriously, no more. I think you're probably right about Mori. He's a genuine expert on folklore, and it's very likely he thinks there's something in it, however he chooses to explain it.'' She looked at Otani with an unexpectedly gentle, almost maternal expression on her young face. "You shouldn't let it get you down, you know, even if it does inspire you to write some quite decent haiku."

Otani grew hot with embarrassment, and mumbled something incomprehensible even to himself. "I could hardly help noticing them," Noriko went on. "I don't know what sort of a state you were in when you left here yesterday but they were all over the floor when I put your bedding away. Don't worry, nobody else has seen them." She went over to the cupboard and took half a dozen sheets of paper from under one of the spare futons stored there. "I write haiku too. I once won a newspaper competition with one of mine. You'd only need to change a word here and there to have a couple of really nice ones to give your wife." She handed them over and then stared at him seriously. "May I make a suggestion?"

"About my haiku? I'd be glad if you would."

"No, no, I mean about this fox business. If you can spare the time, go and see an old lady I know, Mrs. Kazama. She lives not far from my parents."

"Why do you think I should meet this Mrs. Kazama?"

"Well, I don't really know how to describe her, but I've known her all my life and if anyone can put you right about spirit foxes she can. She's a medium, very religious. You wouldn't think it to look at her, but she's incredibly tough. She still goes through all manner of awful training exercises, standing under waterfalls in the middle of winter and so on. Most people who know her think she has second sight. I personally think ninety percent of everything she says is complete gibberish, but I have to admit she's a very impressive person. And she has this terrific reputation for banishing evil spirits. What's the word, exorcising people. If you've really been having hallucinations or whatever I'll bet she can straighten you out."

"I can't begin to imagine how I allowed that young woman to talk me into this," Otani complained to Higashida for at least the third time as their police driver stopped the car and checked with a passer-by that they were on the right road.

"Nearly there, sir," the driver said, winding the window back up. "Apparently it's a house on the corner of a turn-off just round the bend."

"Good. All the same, I wish you'd chosen somebody else to ask. It wasn't absolutely essential to pick a man carrying two buckets of night-soil to put on his vegetable plot."

Otani opened his own window and breathed relatively odor-free air again. They were in the hills about ten miles west of Sumoto, very near the center of the island, in what was neither a village nor open country. During the drive they had hardly ever been out of sight of a house, but everywhere around them was the evidence of small-scale agriculture, on tiny terraces hacked out of the hillsides and under irregular expanses of ramshackle cold frames covered with dirty sheets of glass and, more often, tattered plastic sheeting.

On the way they had passed several neglected-looking Buddhist temples, in any one of which Otani could well imagine the deeply religious but nevertheless sinister-sounding Mrs. Kazama choosing to lurk, and he was convinced they had come to the wrong place when their driver stopped the car outside a small, newish, perfectly ordinary private house with a tiny garden. It was the sort of place any modestly prosperous local tradesman might live in; unremarkable in any way except for the glossy black hire-car parked outside, its driver in his seat immersed in a comic book, his cap and white gloves on the passenger seat beside him.

"Either Mrs. Kazama has another visitor or she's planning to call on the mayor after we leave," Otani said to Higashida as their own driver opened the door for him. Then he spoke to the police driver. "Ask the hire-car man who's inside, would—oh, no need." The front door of the house had been opened and Tadao Mori emerged, gesturing with one hand to his own chauffeur to indicate that he should continue to wait, and to Otani with the forefinger of the other to be quiet.

Otani surveyed him in silence as the lawyer approached. Mori was dressed in the same way as when Otani had called on him. In broad daylight and the open air and in spite of the imposing car at his disposal he seemed less impressive: a shriveled, elderly man with an impatient expression on his face. Nevertheless, his manner was just as confident as before.

"Better late than never, I suppose. Mrs. Kazama was expecting you to turn up some time ago, Inspector. Follow me, but keep your voice down, there's a good fellow. She's at a rather tricky stage in the business of invoking Fudo Myo-o just at present, you see, but it's all right for you to come in. Just you: we can't have your retinue underfoot. They must simply amuse themselves, borrow my driver's comic or something."

Otani turned to Higashida and shrugged eloquently. Higashida bowed slightly in acknowledgement, a hint of a smile on his face, and Mori bustled back toward the door, peremptorily beckoning Otani to follow. The little entry-hall where they took off their shoes was entirely conventional in appearance, but somebody was chanting loudly in a room to the left. The voice was strong, had a nasal quality and could have belonged to a man or a woman. The words were not Japanese and were incomprehensible to Otani, but soon the chant seemed to change, and he noticed Mori nodding with every sign of satisfaction.

"You notice of course that the Middle Spell of Fudo having been satisfactorily completed it's time to move on to the Heart Sutra." In spite of his earlier exaggerated insistence on quiet Mori was speaking in a perfectly normal conversational tone: speaking up if anything to make himself heard over the gabble which was from time to time interspersed with alarming grunts, moans and high-pitched yells.

Mori led the way into a small room dominated by a large and ornately decorated altar with a low platform in front of it, before which was kneeling a little old lady dressed in a white silk kimono. The two men remained near the door, and Otani found himself kneeling without noticing himself do it, Mori following suit. It was hard to credit that so small a body was capable of producing such extraordinary noises, or that its aged owner could possibly shake her clasped hands up and down with such speed and violence. Mori seemed unperturbed by what was going on, but Otani had to restrain himself from intervening when the celebrant, priestess, medium, witch or whatever she was suddenly punched herself with tremendous force several times in the stomach, roaring horribly as she did so.

This climactic stage of her performance chilled Otani's blood but was mercifully brief. Soon the noise level diminished, the chanting was resumed, and within a minute or so stopped altogether. The old lady reached out and struck a brass gong at her side with a short stick, and then turned to her visitors with a sweet smile.

"You must be the policeman the Ito child mentioned," she said to Otani. "Good morning to you. I'm Kazama. You see, I told you he'd be here soon, Mori-sensei, you shouldn't worry so much. I'm glad you arrived before Fudo-sama himself left again. I normally only invoke him when I'm healing, of course."

"Of course," Otani agreed limply. The white silk kimono he associated with corpses was off-putting, but in every other way Mrs. Kazama now looked like any other well-preserved Japanese granny in her seventies. She had plenty of wrinkles but many a woman young enough to be her daughter would have been pleased with a complexion like hers, and her eyes were bright and lively.

"Give me your hand," she said. The altar and platform occupied at least a third of the room so Otani was necessarily near enough for her to reach out and touch him without shifting her position. Her little hand wasn't the typical old lady's loose bundle of skin and bones. It was firm and warm, and her touch filled Otani with an inexplicable sense of peace, so much so that he felt as if he could have knelt there happily for hours like that and was sad when she gently released him, nodding thoughtfully. "You have no real problems. The Suekawa fox has been playing tricks on you out of sheer devilment, but it's not you he's really interested in."

Mori spoke up. "I was asking Mrs. Kazama whether she doesn't agree that the fox has definitely gone too far in murdering the American."

"Do you think he did murder the American, sensei?" The atmosphere seemed so unreal to Otani that he found himself referring to the fox in just as matter-of-fact a way as the other two.

Mrs. Kazama giggled, almost girlishly. "Oh dear, you mustn't call me sensei. I'm just an ordinary old woman. Well, yes, I think the fox did do it, and I also think it's high time he was sent back to Izumo where he belongs. It's a good job the Tokiwa Inn's not far from the Inari Shrine. The veil's always pretty thin at shrines."

"The veil?" Otani still felt calm and relaxed, but completely out of his depth. It was the lawyer who, after tut-tutting at his ignorance, enlightened him.

"The veil between the worlds, Inspector. I must say it is tiresome having to explain every little thing to you. Thanks to the austerities she has practiced for most of her life Mrs. Kazama is able to pass between the worlds more or less wherever she is with the aid of sutras and other holy texts, but I think that she would be the first to agree that even for her it is much easier to do so where the veil is particularly thin."

Mrs. Kazama nodded in casual agreement, as though they were discussing some humdrum everyday chore.

"And that's at shrines?" Otani was anxious to keep up.

"Well, of course, mountains and waterfalls are best," she said. "But there are lots of other places. Near big rocks or old trees with god-bodies in them, for example. Some shrines are particularly close to the other world, you must have felt it yourself, surely, at the Grand Shrines at Ise, or the Itsukushima Shrine at Miyajima near Hiroshima?"

"I suppose there is something special about those places, yes."

"Gracious me, you *are* a hard nut to crack, aren't you?" Mori cried merrily. "Well, the shrine in Sumoto isn't anything special, and that greedy clod of a priest doesn't help matters much, but even so it *is* an Inari Shrine, and therefore useful when it's a fox-spirit that's giving trouble."

"Um, this is a very ignorant question, I know," Otani began in a timid way, "but presumably the fox had to work *through* somebody to kill the American?"

111

"Oh yes, of course." Mori gazed at him in obvious pity, and Otani sighed.

"I do wish you'd explained that when we met before. Well, that being so, could I ask you, or you, Mrs. Kazama, who that might have been? You say Mrs. Suekawa senior is the one who is actually possessed by the fox, but she's very old, very frail and never goes out. I don't see how the fox could have used her to kill a healthy, strong young man."

Mrs. Kazama again directed her soul-cleansing smile at him. "You haven't *completely* understood. She brought the fox from Izumo in the first place but now it's attached to the whole household, so it could have used anybody living or even visiting there, you see."

Otani smiled ruefully. "Oh dear, so I'm no better off than I was before, am I?"

"Nonsense, man, of course you are," Mori insisted. "In the first place, you have at last got it in your thick head that the fox did it. And now that you have, the obvious thing is to *ask* the wretched creature who it used."

Otani rubbed his mouth to conceal another smile. "I rather doubt if it would tell me," he said then.

"Perhaps not," Mrs. Kazama said. "But it might tell me. And if not me, it will certainly tell Fudo-sama."

Chapter 15

"**G**OOD NEWS, I TRUST?" THE SURFACE OF INSPECTOR Saburo Takada's desk was as empty of papers as it had been the first time Otani had seen it. The inspector was in uniform, and still had about him the indefinably wary air Otani had noticed when Takada told him he was to ring the prefectural commander's office as soon as possible.

Otani shrugged. The news would be all over headquarters by now so there was no reason not to tell Takada. "I don't know, quite honestly," he said. "I've been expecting a transfer, but I'd taken it for granted it would be farther afield than my own doorstep. It seems they want me to take over the Nada divisional D.I. job."

Takada looked gravely pleased. "Allow me to congratulate you. As one who has shouldered the responsibilities of a divisional command for a very long time—and thank goodness Assistant Inspector Kuroda is due back at his desk tomorrow—I believe you will find your new duties both more challenging and, dare I say it, more *down-to-earth* than those of a headquarters staff post."

"Yes, very likely. I shall also have to brush up my riot-control techniques judging by the way students up and down the country are behaving lately. The Nada patch includes the

Kobe University campus and several other colleges of one sort and another.''

"Does it indeed? Perhaps I should add my commiserations as well, then. Fortunately, and whether by luck or judgment it is not for me to say, I have been able to keep all that sort of thing well under control here.'' Since the entire island of Awaji boasted not a single institution of higher education Otani kept his mouth firmly closed, and after a moment Takada asked the question he was expecting. "Ah . . . this means, I presume, that you will be setting off post-haste back to Kobe? I shall of course escort you in my own car to the ferry at any time convenient to you.''

"You're very kind, but there's no immediate urgency. The effective date for me to take over in Nada Division is the Monday after next, and I shall only need a couple of days to clear my desk in Kobe. So I'll be able to wind up the case here before I leave.''

There was rather a long pause before Takada responded, "I see . . . I had rather imagined that you would have wished—''

"It would go very much against the grain for me to turn over a case to somebody else unless there was no alternative, Inspector. And in any case I expect to have completed my investigation here and be in a position to recommend an arrest within the next twenty-four hours or so. Maybe two.''

"*Two*? Two *arrests*?''

"That's right,'' Otani said calmly as Takada goggled at him. "The monthly ennichi festival at the Inari Shrine is tomorrow evening, isn't it? I wouldn't want to miss that, in any case. I'm told your friend Horiuchi has built it up into a really impressive occasion.'' Takada seemed to have been struck dumb and Otani spoke again, quietly, but with steel in his voice. "I presume he has told you about my conversation with him at Iwaya? The one you didn't want me to have with him? Given you an edited version, at least? Let me put your mind at rest on one important point, Inspector. There was a stage when I thought otherwise, and there are still good grounds to do so, but I can now reassure you that you're not one of the people I have it in mind to arrest. What

114

I do want is for you to tell me what became of that little fox image you had in your possession.''

While Otani was speaking it was as if Takada aged visibly, and by the time he paused the older man's face was drained of color, and his mouth was working painfully. "I . . . fox image?''

"You didn't think anybody would ever notice, did you? You've been both foolish and rather unlucky, Inspector. In addition to the earlier folly you've been trying to cover up with criminal recklessness, I mean. Unlucky because Patrolman Higashida is an extremely intelligent and versatile young officer and he happened to be the one who responded to the report that Kington's body had been found. Foolish to assign him to me as an assistant rather than keeping him at arm's length from me as you could have done.'' Otani took out his cigarettes, lit one and sat back more comfortably in the easy chair, his eyes never leaving Takada's face.

"No, there's no need to say anything yet. I'll explain a few things to you first. They say the first thing you should do when you've got yourself into a hole is stop digging, so think hard about what you're going to tell me when the time comes. This conversation is off the record, possibly the last one I shall have with you on those terms. I probably owe you that much consideration as a senior colleague. It suits me too, because I can get a few things off my own chest that I wouldn't necessarily want to see in my formal report. I don't think you're really an evil man, Takada. You're pompous and conceited, and you're stupid. Even so, you fooled me for a while when I first arrived here, by giving such a clever performance. Every time I asked myself how it was possible you could be so totally uninterested in the murder of a foreigner on your own territory I reminded myself you're within a few months of retirement, and that it wasn't unreasonable to imagine a man as idle and self-satisfied as you represented yourself to be shoving anything awkward somebody else's way. But in fact you've been quite a busy little bee, haven't you?''

By now Takada was gripping the edge of his desk, so tightly that Otani could see the whiteness the pressure created

115

near the ends of his fingernails. He had, however, recovered the power of speech. "Off the record, you say, and then add impertinence to your intolerable interference in my personal affairs. Well, off the record, Otani, you are an arrogant man, puffed up because you seem to have succeeded in ingratiating yourself with our superiors. If you play your cards right in Nada no doubt you can expect promotion and a fat job in Tokyo in a few years. Of course a gaijin-loving big-city operator and office politician like you looks down on somebody like me, just a steady old country policeman, a patriotic Japanese content to do his work and enjoy the respect of his friends. Well, you may be clever, but you're out of your depth here, let me tell you."

Otani's face had remained expressionless throughout, and when he replied his tone was neutral. "Good. That's cleared the air. Now we can get down to business. Tell me what you did with the little china fox."

"So far as I know, this object which seems to obsess you is under lock and key with the other evidence."

"No it isn't. I've already told you I know you took it."

"I did remove it for a short while to examine it, certainly. Then I replaced it."

"You replaced it, yes, but not until the day after the murder, and then with a similar one. One I wouldn't be surprised to find that Horiuchi provided. I imagine he was horrified when you told him what you'd done with the original. It was easy for him to get hold of a replacement. They sell them at the shrine."

Takada raised his eyes heavenwards and managed a reasonable attempt at a tolerant smile. "I don't know if you'd care to explain what this preposterous tale is supposed to be leading up to?"

"By all means. I doubt if you expected Kington to be murdered, but when you heard about it you immediately guessed who must have done it, and set about laying a false trail to divert suspicion from that person. You knew that Gary Wilson detested Craig Kington, and you therefore planted the fox in his room intending me to find it, assume it was one of a pair, and look no further for the murderer. The

116

young man Wilson is obviously in a precarious psychological state and given time I suppose he might in fact have gone over the edge and killed Kington."

"So you found a fox in his room, did you?"

"Not *a* fox, Inspector, *the* fox. But of course I didn't realize that at the time. I had to check it against the photographs before I could be sure. I'd already noticed that the one in the locker didn't quite match the picture Higashida had taken of the scene. It was the same size but they're all painted by hand, you see. Only a few strokes of the brush but no two could possibly come out exactly alike. Even I could spot the differences, and of course the forensic lab will be able to spell them out precisely."

"I have only your unsupported word for all this. Where is this other fox now, the one you allege to be the original? I should like to see for myself."

Otani reached toward his jacket pocket, hesitated, took his hand away, hesitated again and finally fished out the little ceramic fox whose shape it had been difficult to conceal. "Well, I'm not sure . . ." he began as he handed it over. Then he sat still, making no attempt to stop him as Takada stood up, threw the fox to the tiled floor and shattered it by stamping on it before grinding the pieces under his heel.

"What will you do now?" Otani inquired. "Doctor the photographs or claim they didn't 'come out?' " There was a bright spot of color in each of Takada's cheeks and he was breathing heavily, but he said nothing.

"I was about to say, before you obligingly confirmed my conclusion, that it was of course possible that Higashida himself could have interfered with the evidence by making the substitution. Might even conceivably have been the one who killed Kington in the first place. He had a motive. His girlfriend knew the dead man and had possibly slept with him. No, Takada, it's too late for you to take refuge in that theory now. Not after that little performance. A pity you didn't give me a chance to explain that the fox you just smashed was bought for me at the shrine by Higashida an hour or so ago for that purpose. The right one's in a safe place. Now, why don't you just tell me who you're protecting?"

"Wouldn't you like to know?" Takada was still on his feet and swaying slightly. This time he almost snarled his reply, and if Otani had still been in his earlier suggestive state he might have peeped surreptitiously to see if the tip of a bushy white tail was protruding from the inspector's trouser-bottoms. As it was he took a last, satisfying drag at his cigarette and stubbed it out with deliberate care into the ashtray on the desk.

"Oh, I *do* know. I said I want you to tell me. That's not at all the same thing."

"You're bluffing."

"Now why would I want to do a thing like that?"

"Because you've come to a dead end as I knew you would, and you're hoping against hope you can trick me into compromising myself."

"Come now, be reasonable. By smashing that worthless copy you've already in effect just admitted you took the fox from the locker Higashida put it in with the other evidence, Kington's clothes and the contents of his pockets and so on, and left it in Wilson's room to implicate him."

"I have made no such admission. I have smashed nothing. You can prove nothing." Takada bent down and began to pick up the fragments of china from the floor, putting them one by one into his pocket.

"Sit down, Inspector," Otani said quietly. "I'll clear up the mess myself." Takada looked at him and then slowly straightened up and slumped into his chair, all the fight gone out of him at last. "I'm glad your deputy's due back in the morning. Kuroda, I think you said his name is. That probably means he'll be back in Sumoto later today and can relieve you more or less right away. In any case, I want you to go home and stay there until further notice. Now we can do this the easy way, or the hard way. The easy way is for you to take a few days' sick leave. The hard way would be for me to get on the phone to Kobe and advise the commander to suspend you from duty with immediate effect pending a full disciplinary inquiry. He'll do it if I ask him, I assure you."

"What does it matter? I'm ruined anyway." Speaking in

little more than a whisper, Takada looked and sounded like a broken old man.

"Not necessarily. Finished, yes, I think so, but I don't seek your ruin, Inspector. A sympathetic doctor wouldn't even have to bend the truth much if he were to recommend bringing your retirement forward on health grounds. You'd still get your retirement allowances. And as you say, you have—whether you deserve it or not—the respect of many friends here apart from Horiuchi, who has used and exploited you. Be sensible, I beg you. Go home, and keep yourself strictly to yourself until this is all over. I'm not going to stop you unless you make me."

Otani did clear up the mess of broken china on the floor, and it was he who ordered the inspector's car to be brought to take him home. He went along too, and explained quietly to the concerned but dignified lady who was Mrs. Takada that her husband had been under a great deal of pressure and had collapsed in his office. His doctor should see him, of course, but in Otani's opinion the inspector had simply been overdoing it and would be quite himself again after a period of complete rest.

Mrs. Takada was much relieved when the doctor left the house a couple of hours later having confirmed Otani's amateur diagnosis and administered a sedative.

"What a charming man that inspector from Kobe is," she said as she sat beside her husband with her embroidery; but he seemed not to hear her. Perhaps, she thought, he was already asleep.

Chapter 16

OTANI SLID THE DOOR TO BEHIND HIM, WALKED STRAIGHT over to the window of his room and flung himself into one of the two easy-chairs there, strongly tempted to check out of the Tokiwa without more ado and find somewhere else to stay. The proprietor himself had been lying in wait for him on his return and subjected Otani to a long, involved and effusive monologue.

Otani now liked him even less than he had after their only previous encounter. Suekawa was as oily and servile as before, but there had been about his manner this time, a knowing slyness which left Otani feeling soiled, and disgusted both with himself and with Suekawa. Not that the wretched man had actually said anything of substance. All his convoluted courtesies had amounted to was a repetitious explanation that his mother was a very old lady who now and then wandered in her mind and had to be spoken to rather sharply, profuse apologies for the inconvenience to the honored guest and smug assurances that he, Suekawa, had spared no effort in preparing an evening meal which might conceivably make up to some slight extent for the inspector's having been deprived of his breakfast.

It was Suekawa's greasy little eyes, never at rest but never quite leaving Otani's face, that had conveyed a completely different message. This was to the effect that he either knew or guessed that his wife had made a play for Otani and that he took a prurient pleasure in speculating about what might or might not have passed between them. Might even, Otani thought, have somehow spied on them in the bath. Suekawa struck him as being the sort of man who would enjoy contriving peepholes here and there, easy enough in an old place like the Tokiwa. Otani thought he would also be quite capable of being excited by the idea of his hot-blooded wife making love with other men and even conniving at her adventures.

He stirred restlessly in the chair. It was half past six. It would take him literally no more than a minute or two to bundle up his few belongings in the furoshiki and another five to pay his bill and be off to the first decent-looking inn. If they couldn't feed him there he could find something to eat at a restaurant easily enough. If the worst came to the worst he could spend the night in an armchair at police headquarters. The more he thought about it the more unendurable the prospect of another night in—

"Hello. Look what I've got here."

Just too late his door was unceremoniously opened and Noriko came in with an enormous, fully laden tray. It turned out to be one of two, and when she had somehow contrived to find room on the table for the array of dishes of various shapes and sizes they both gazed down at the banquet with a certain awe. All the predictable things were there: opulent chunks of raw bream, tuna and octopus arranged as *sashimi*, a delicate broth with shelled clams and seaweed, one of the grilled crayfish he had enjoyed particularly on the first evening, a steaming vegetable dish and delicate platters of hors d'oeuvres. There were other, more unusual items, too: a thick fillet steak already cut into bite-sized pieces, a baked potato nestling in silver foil, short lengths of leek wrapped in wafer-thin slices of pork, and most surprising of all, an opened but full bottle of Chivas Regal Scotch whisky.

"Actually, I was just about to check out," Otani said at last. "But in the circumstances . . . um, Miss Ito, could you possibly stay for a while and help me eat this?" Noriko smiled cheerfully, took a zabuton from the corner of the room and settled herself at the table without hesitation. She just happened to have a spare pair of disposable wooden chopsticks with her.

"He did apologize because I had to go without breakfast this morning and said he'd made up for it, but this is ridiculous."

"Funny you should say you were planning to check out," Noriko said, then ducked her head in a sketchy bow and chanted the ritual *"Itadakimasu!"*, after which she began to tuck in. Two mouthfuls later she added, "I'm leaving myself tonight."

"Any particular reason?"

"Mrs. Kazama rang me up and told me to. *And* both she and old Mori got on to my parents, *and* they got on to me. Everyone's in a tremendous tizzy, it seems. What did you make of the old lady, by the way?"

"I was enormously impressed by her and I'm more than grateful to you for suggesting I should go to see her. She did, er, straighten me out about spirit foxes, as you put it. But please go on, why are she and Mori—and your parents—so insistent that you should leave at once?"

Noriko shrugged and helped herself to a piece of steak. "They seem to think I'm in some kind of danger here. Superstitious nonsense, but I'm ready for a change anyway and they're in such a state I thought I might as well humor them. Want some of this whisky?"

Otani shook his head. "No thanks. I normally only ever drink whisky after I've wound up a case. I broke my own rule the other night and look what it did for me. I ended up . . . writing haiku."

There was a quirky little smile on Noriko's face. "So you did. Are you really going to check out today?"

"Well, we're eating this amazing *gochiso* so I might as well have the night's lodging that goes with it. But I'll definitely move tomorrow." He made a gallant little gesture. "No point in staying if you aren't going to be here." Noriko's small face began to scrunch itself up into a scowl and Otani feared for a moment that once more he had thoughtlessly offended her, but she stopped herself and relaxed again. "Don't misunderstand me," he went on. "I haven't by any means sorted everything out yet, but I do see a gleam of light at the end of the tunnel, thanks to your help and advice. And I really mean it when I say that this will be a pretty dismal place without you around."

"What, even with old Suekawa laying on a meal like this and her ladyship after you with her tongue hanging out?" Otani winced at her crudity but said nothing and after a while Noriko herself colored slightly. "Sorry, I keep forgetting you're this VIP official. Oh, by the way, talking of officials, I nearly forgot. Phone message for you from Inspector Takada's number two. Kuroki? Kuroiwa?"

"Kuroda."

"That's the name, yes. He's just got back to Sumoto and wants to come over this evening to see you."

"Really? What time did he ring?"

"About fifteen, twenty minutes ago. I got to the phone just as I was going to bring all this stuff up here for you. I told him you were just about to eat your supper. Right, he said. Tell him I'll be over about seven forty-five."

"You weren't sure of his name. You don't know Assistant Inspector Kuroda, then?"

"No. The only policeman I know around here apart from you is Higashida."

"I see. Look, this is none of my business, but—"

"No. If you're about to say what I think you are, it isn't. I'm quite capable of making up my own mind about our friendly local snooper, thank you." Noriko's quick grin took the sharpness out of her reply and Otani gave her no more than a sidelong glance before reaching out for a chunk of the white meat of the crayfish.

He was to regret that succulent morsel whenever he remembered the occasion thereafter, for he hadn't quite conveyed it to his mouth when an eerie screech from outside froze him in position with hand upraised. At the same time the sliding *fusuma* door to his left first seemed to bulge inwards and then sprang from its runner grooves and crashed down among the dishes littering the table. In the doorway like an avenging fury stood old Mrs. Suekawa gibbering incomprehensibly, a wicked-looking kitchen knife quivering in one claw-like hand.

When Otani's brain began to function again a fraction of a second later his first conscious reaction was one of shame that Noriko had moved much faster than he. She was already on her feet by the window brandishing one of the lightweight rattan chairs in the stereotyped pose of the circus lion-tamer. It was an eminently sensible thing to do, since in that position Noriko was well out of the old woman's reach. Otani was tempted to follow suit but then reluctantly concluded that something more positive was required of him and that an experienced senior police officer trained in unarmed combat ought to be capable of disarming a crazed old woman half his size and getting on for twice his age.

It turned out to be not quite so simple as it ought to have been, mainly because he twice inadvertently slipped, once on a length of leek and once in the dregs of the clam soup which had otherwise soaked into the tatami mat. The old lady was herself astonishingly wiry and agile and Otani had no wish to hurt her, but even so it was of course a very one-sided contest and within less than half a minute the knife was safely on the floor in a far corner of the room and Mrs. Suekawa was flopping helplessly in a neat professional arm-lock.

Noriko put the chair down and approached warily, scooping up a tumbler and the bottle of whisky which was miraculously still upright. With a hand that shook a little she poured out a couple of inches of whisky and drank half of it neat in a single mouthful. Then, coughing and spluttering, she held the glass out to Otani.

"No, thanks, I'll have one later," he said, shaking his head. "Go and get some help, please."

Still half choking on the whisky, Noriko didn't manage to answer coherently, but the hand she was flapping toward the wrecked doorway was sufficiently eloquent. Turning his head that way Otani saw a dramatic tableau consisting of a dapper, sardonic-looking man in his thirties elegantly turned out in police uniform, a gaping Higashida and a crumpled heap which had to be an unconscious Etsuko Suekawa.

"It was extraordinary," Assistant Inspector Kuroda said after he had introduced himself and they had taken the now pathetic, feebly weeping old woman to a nearby room where Noriko had hurriedly laid out a futon for Otani to lower her gently down on. Then Noriko had gone back to attend to Etsuko Suekawa. "She took one look at the three of you and fainted on the spot. It was like Pavlova in the Dying Swan." Otani hadn't the slightest idea what Kuroda was talking about but liked the look of him all the same. "Ah, here she is now. Feeling better, madam?"

In fact, although Etsuko Suekawa was wearing a splendid kimono predominantly a warm burgundy in color, she looked haggard, somehow shrunken, and ill. Guided by Noriko to a spare zabuton she collapsed rather than lowered herself on to it and stared dully at her mother-in-law, ignoring the three men in the room.

"Higashida," Otani said quietly, "you'd better go and find the old lady's son and send him up here. Also, get hold of a clean towel, pillowcase or something and wrap that knife up loosely in it. Don't touch it yourself more than you can help." He darted a quick glance at Noriko's pale face. "Perhaps you'd be kind enough to go with the officer and give him a hand. Then the two of you might as well wait downstairs."

When the two young people had left the room with quite as much alacrity as Otani had expected he turned to Kuroda. "Well, I need hardly say how grateful I am to see you here this evening. Not quite the straightforward return to your desk you were expecting, I'm afraid." He gestured unobtrusively toward Etsuko Suekawa, who sat motionless and apparently oblivious to anything except the spectacle of her mother-in-law on the futon. She twitched and made curious little moaning sounds from time to time but otherwise seemed to be sleeping. "I won't go any further at the moment into what I told you in my note, but I can confirm that you're going to be acting for Inspector Takada for some time."

Kuroda nodded, a hint of a smile on his darkly handsome face. It was not lost on Otani, but his own expression was unreadable as he continued. "Even before this, um, bit of excitement I had planned to check out of the Tokiwa this evening. The maid I sent downstairs with Higashida just now doesn't sleep in, and in any case I believe this is her last working day in this job. Her name's Noriko Ito, by the way. And there are no other guests. So unless we decide to make other arrangements, that means that only the proprietor, his wife and his mother will be sleeping here."

"I suppose we ought to get a doctor to look at the patient?"

Otani nodded. "I'm sure you're right to refer to her as a patient, and yes, of course she must be examined. I expect if she's given a sedative she'll be as good as gold for quite a long time. On the other hand about half an hour ago she was waving a knife about with what certainly looked like murderous intent. And the younger Mrs. Suekawa has had a very nasty shock. I don't think it would be fair to her to expect her to watch over her mother-in-law all night long, and frankly I don't think we can rely too heavily on her husband. It's up to you, of course, you're in the operational command chair now. But I've been watching this crisis develop, and my advice would be to get the doctor to admit the old lady to a private hospital room under observation for a few days. Get specialist reports—yes, what is it, Higashida?"

"Sir, I'm sorry to disturb you, sir, but there are two visitors for you."

"Visitors? For me? Who are they?"

"Well, sir, actually, it's Mori-sensei, sir. The lawyer. And Mrs. Kazama. They insist on seeing you, sir. In fact—"

"Out of our way, young man!" Mori brushed Higashida aside and surveyed the scene from the open doorway. "Hah! Just as I thought. Assistant Inspector Kuroda, is it not? Good evening to you. And to you, Inspector. You seem to have contrived to keep the poltroon Takada at a distance. Well done." He turned and boomed over his shoulder. "Come in, Mrs. Kazama, come in! We have timed our arrival well. There's work for you here, dear lady!"

Chapter 17

"**I**'M NOT ABSOLUTELY SURE," OTANI SAID OFFHAND-edly, "but I rather think it's the Middle Spell of Fudo." Even in his confused state of mind he relished the look on the face of Assistant Inspector Kuroda. "Mrs. Kazama is a much respected medium and exorcist, and my guess is that she's invoking the Lord Fudo as a preliminary to dealing with old Mrs. Suekawa's fox once and for all." The strange, inhuman voice which had so disconcerted him when he called at Mrs. Kazama's house that morning was clearly audible in the room across the corridor where he and Kuroda were sitting alone, having been briskly banished by Mrs. Kazama herself. Now, however, he found it reassuring and with a little mental effort could experience again something of the inner peace he had known while Mrs. Kazama held his hand.

Kuroda shifted uneasily on his cushion and cleared his throat. "With all due respect, sir, I'm not at all happy about allowing Mori and this Mrs. Kazama to be in there unsuper-vised with those two women, and in any case . . ."

"And in any case you're beginning to wonder whether I'm off my head too. I don't blame you in the least. All you've had to go on so far is my note and whatever Higashida may have told you on your way to this madhouse. Even so, let me handle this for just another half an hour or so, will you? I accept full responsibility. I promise you we'll get that doctor here immediately after that, and meantime let me try to put you in the picture.''

"Well . . .''

"Try to pay no attention to those yelps and grunts. We may not have the remotest idea what Mrs. Kazama thinks she's doing, but she knows, I assure you. All right, Inspector Takada first.''

"He's not really ill, is he?''

Otani looked at Kuroda's intelligent face and decided it was safe to be frank with him. "Not in the ordinary sense of the word. I had to side-line him though, and as I implied a while ago I doubt if he'll be back soon or indeed at all.'' He paused, then put the question bluntly. "Did you know he was on the take from the priest Horiuchi?''

Kuroda took his time over replying. "Not specifically, no. I've been here less than a year and I've only had my doubts about him during the past few months.''

"What about Horiuchi himself? Been to any of these monthly ennichi fairs of his, have you?''

"A couple, and I've met him once or twice. He's a nasty piece of work, and so are some of the characters who turn up at the fairs.''

"They'll be the bosses who organize the *tekiya*, the hucksters and stallholders. They come from Kobe, and Horiuchi goes over there to see them and their superiors quite often. He went the other day and I had him tailed and pictures were taken of him calling in at a *yakuza* syndicate office. Takada knew all about it and turned a blind eye for a consideration.''

"A blind eye to what, for heaven's sake? The monthly fair's popular in Sumoto and I dare say the hucksters do all right out of it, but it's hardly the big time, surely?''

"No, of course it isn't. What it does do is give one of the Kobe syndicates a toe-hold they've been wanting here for a long time. And with their muscle behind him Horiuchi has developed a sophisticated protection racket and become in effect the yakuza boss for Awaji.'' Otani paused and cocked his head. The chanting was continuing but had become quieter and more even.

"All's well, she seems to have moved on to a sutra. Yes, well, I don't just mean raking in payoffs from all the hotspring inns and bars and restaurants and so forth, though that must net a tidy income if, as I suspect, Horiuchi has pretty well buttoned up the whole island. No, I'm talking about substantial sums extorted from businessmen who don't like the idea of their property being burned down or their dirty little secrets exposed. They don't pay 'insurance' or hushmoney, oh dear no, they make generous donations to the Inari Shrine, a charitable foundation. All above-board and openly accounted for in their business tax returns. To be fair to him I doubt very much if Takada realized the extent of what's been going on, and I'm quite sure you didn't." The expression on Kuroda's face convinced Otani that he was right about that at least.

"The murder of the American terrified Takada, because he was convinced either Horiuchi or his wife had done it. The Horiuchis cultivated Takada, you see, entertained him, invited him to visit their luxurious house. Fed his vanity, made him think he really was a big shot. But he isn't an unobservant man, and at some stage he twigged that Horiuchi's wife was having an affair with Kington."

Kuroda nodded. "If anybody knew about Kington's private life, it would be Takada. He was absolutely obsessed with those two Americans. Hated the idea of their being here at all. I know he was forever snooping around them, asking their neighbors about their movements and so on."

"I'm not surprised to hear that. Anyway, when Kington's body was found so near the Horiuchi house he jumped to the conclusion that either the priest had found out about the affair and killed the American—Horiuchi's also a fanatical antiforeigner—or that the wife had because she was afraid the priest was about to find out. Did Higashida tell you about the little fox image in Kington's hands?"

"Yes."

"Well, Takada knew it had been photographed. So he hit on the crazy idea of purloining it and planting it in the other

129

American's room to divert suspicion away from the Horiuchis and implicate Wilson. It's hard to credit the idea that he'd try to pin a murder on to an innocent man just to get rid of him, but by that stage I think he really was probably a bit unhinged. Anyway, it dawned on him a bit late that questions would be asked if a piece of evidence disappeared from police custody, so he got hold of a duplicate fox and substituted it. It was almost identical to the original but unfortunately for Takada not quite. When he realized I was on to him he fell apart and saw the force of my suggestion that he might consider having a nervous breakdown and going for early retirement on health grounds.''

"I see. Thank you, I'm reasonably clear about that part now. So you don't think either of the Horiuchis killed the American, then?''

"No, I don't. It was certainly a possibility that had to be considered, if only because of the dog.''

"Dog?''

"You obviously don't know your Sherlock Holmes. The Horiuchis have a very noisy guard dog, and it didn't bark in the night. So somebody it knew must have been around when Kington was killed—''

"Make haste, both of you! The moment of truth is near!'' It was Mori, beckoning them furiously from the open doorway.

As he and Kuroda followed Mori into the room Otani shivered involuntarily and felt goose-pimples rise on his arms. Mrs. Kazama looked quite serene on her zabuton, facing the tokonoma alcove in which was displayed nothing but a commonplace hanging scroll Otani hadn't noticed earlier during all the excitement. The painting on it was indifferently executed and inappropriate to the season, but he doubted if it bothered Mrs. Kazama, who was chanting the Heart Sutra not in the penetrating nasal tones he had heard her use before but with an extraordinary driving momentum. What froze his blood was the look on the face of old Mrs. Suekawa, who was sitting bolt upright on the bedding Noriko had laid for her.

It was quite unlike the murderous fury of her expression when she had burst in on the two of them clutching the knife. That had been both ugly and frightening enough, but all the same something comprehensible. This infinitely sly, twisted grin was somehow inhuman; something that sat with terrifying incongruity on the face of what ought to have been a harmless, rather pathetic old woman. She shot a glance of what Otani afterward thought of as almost friendly complicity in the direction of the two police officers, and then glared balefully at Mrs. Kazama.

"YOU DON'T SCARE ME WITH THAT RUBBISH, YOU SILLY OLD BAG!"

Tadao Mori's only reaction to the hoarse shout that issued from Mrs. Suekawa's mouth was to look at the old woman over the top of his glasses with keen interest, but both Otani and Kuroda flinched.

"YOU'LL HAVE TO DO BETTER THAN THAT," the voice shouted then. "YOU'RE NOT WANTED HERE. BUGGER OFF! GO AND STUFF YOURSELF!"

This time Mrs. Kazama interrupted her chanting and glanced briefly toward the quivering figure on the bedding. "Getting a bit too hot for you, is it?" she inquired. "Well, I've got some questions for you, but watch your language. We want none of your filthy talk here."

"NOT IN FRONT OF YOUR FINE FRIENDS, THAT IT? OR THIS DIRTY OLD SKINFLINT?" Mori clearly interpreted this last as a reference to himself and beamed in acknowledgment, but Mrs. Kazama tut-tutted.

"Now I've already warned you once. Any more of that sort of thing and you'll pay for it. Right, now we haven't got all night to bother with you, so let's get on with it. You've been well looked after here all these years, so why all this wicked nonsense all of a sudden?"

"She's quite right, you know, you mustn't talk to the lady like that." Briefly the face was again that of confused, frightened old woman and Mrs. Suekawa spoke in an ordinary, quavering voice; but then the muscles of her face seemed to seize up again and the harsh, hectoring voice once more took over. "AND YOU CAN SHUT YOUR FACE TOO, YOU

SCHEMING OLD HAG! LOOKED AFTER? A FEW SCRAPINGS FROM THE KITCHEN WHEN THAT SNIVELING BASTARD'S BACK WAS TURNED? CALL HIM A SON? FEELING UP THAT LITTLE SPY'S BUM EVERY CHANCE HE GOT TILL SHE KICKED HIM IN THE BALLS? SERVE HIM RIGHT!''

Otani gazed at the old woman in pity and fascination. It was as though she was literally possessed, that she had nothing whatsoever to do with the production of the filthy insults that issued from her mouth, yet that in brief intervals of lucidity the poor old creature retained enough awareness of what was happening to her to try feebly to protest. Mrs. Kazama apparently decided that the conversation was not yet proceeding satisfactorily, swung back to face the hanging scroll again and embarked once more on what Otani now definitely recognized as the invocation of the deity Fudo. The fox, as it now seemed quite reasonable to think of it, was not pleased. Every few seconds it drowned even Mrs. Kazama's powerful voice by shouting some crude gibe or obscenity, and once it sang a whole verse of a vulgar song. Eventually, though, its mounting discomfort found expression.

"ALL RIGHT ALL RIGHT ALL RIGHT! GIVE IT A REST!''

Mrs. Kazama took her time over desisting. "Very well, then, but only as long as you behave yourself. If you do, the Lord Fudo might let you go back to Izumo where you belong. Now then, I want the truth. You've had a generous mistress but not content with that you've been bothering the others in this place, haven't you?''

For the first time since he re-entered the room Otani felt those piercing eyes on him again, and shivered as the horrible, relentless voice cackled at him "HAD A BIT OF FUN WITH THAT ONE, ANYWAY! HIM AND THAT FAT TART!''

Mrs. Kazama now sounded seriously irritated, but still very much in command of the proceedings. "For the last time, *that will do*! Now we all know you killed that poor young man, but the question is, who's going to get the blame for it, eh?''

As she was upbraiding the fox once more Otani suddenly went cold for a completely different reason and backed out into the corridor, pulling Mori after him by the sleeve. *"Where is she?"* he hissed at the lawyer.

"What a time to bother me with questions! Here we are about to learn what you very much want to know and—where's who?"

"The daughter, you blithering old fool! Etsuko! When did she go out of the room? Why the hell did you let her go?"

Mori fastidiously disengaged Otani's hand from his sleeve. "In view of the language we've all been subjected to I will overlook the intemperate way you choose to express yourself. I can't exactly remember when the younger Mrs. Suekawa left the room. There has been too much going on, and I would point out that you have only just noticed her absence yourself. Why ask me where she has gone? To lie down in privacy, perhaps? She has obviously been under considerable strain . . ." Mori abandoned the sentence when he realized that Otani was on his way downstairs, shrugged and went back into the room where Mrs. Kazama was continuing to interrogate an increasingly sullen and taciturn fox.

"Definitely not, sir," Higashida insisted. "Miss Ito and I have been here in the kitchen all the time since we came downstairs. We'd definitely have heard the sliding door if she'd gone out that way. And we weren't in your room more than a few minutes before that. Just long enough to collect your own things together for you—they're in the entrance hall wrapped up in your furoshiki."

Otani snapped his fingers repeatedly in exasperation. The three of them had searched the inn and found no trace of Etsuko Suekawa. "And you say her husband had already gone out? How could he have cleared up so quickly after preparing that colossal meal?" Without waiting for an answer he swung round to confront Noriko. "You say he always goes to the same bar every evening?"

"Most evenings. I'd be surprised if he isn't there now."

"Higashida. You know where it is, I presume. Get round there at the double and bring him back here immediately. If he doesn't want to come, arrest him. Fetch a uniformed man from the nearest police box to help if necessary. No, wait a minute. Before you do that, ring headquarters and tell them to organize a doctor and an ambulance. A senior doctor, preferably somebody who knows something about senile dementia. And I'd better take charge of that knife the old woman was waving about.''

Chapter 18

"OH, ONE VERY RARELY HAS THE SATISFACTION OF being able to tie up all the loose ends in a case," Otani said. "Still, there's always a chance we shall pick up a trace of her somewhere one of these days." The two men were walking slowly down the main shopping street, Kuroda looking rather dashing in a tweed sports jacket and whipcord trousers, Otani unobtrusive in his nondescript suit, his raincoat flapping open. It wasn't really cold but he thought he might be glad of the extra layer later on.

Kuroda rubbed a hand over his chin. "No harm in hoping, sir. But tens of thousands of Japanese 'evaporate' every year and precious few of them ever materialize again. We've notified all police boxes in Awaji and checked with all the various ferry companies as well as the one in Iwaya. No use. Why should anybody notice one out of probably hundreds of housewives in their thirties using the ferries every day? She could be at the other end of Japan by now. At least the old lady's in safe hands. Good of Mori to pay for the private room."

"Yes. Interesting, wasn't it? The doctor's report."

"Fascinating. Mrs. Kazama obviously did a fine job. I'm quite looking forward to getting to know her better. I meant

135

to tell you that Mori rang me while you were writing up your report this afternoon.''

''Oh? What did he want?''

''It took him a long time to get to the point, but what it amounted to was that he wants to lay certain legal information before us, as he put it. I've arranged for him to come and see us both first thing in the morning. I know you want to be on a ferry around midday, but there'll be plenty of time for you to hear what he has to say before we drive you to Iwaya. I'd appreciate your reactions.''

''Thanks. Glad to sit in.''

''He rambled on rather amusingly for some time about Mrs. Kazama. She's the widow of a doctor, it seems. Been developing her spiritual talents for donkey's years. Educated woman herself, according to Mori. He said she once told him she went to a school in Tokyo run by English missionaries. Round about the time of the First World War, it must have been. She told Mori the experience left her with an equal loathing for Christianity and English food. Incidentally, talking of missionaries, Gary Wilson's gone back to Tokyo. The American Embassy rang to say he'd lodged his passport with them until we give him formal permission to leave the country.''

Otani made a sound halfway between a chuckle and a snort. The more he saw of Kuroda the more he liked his easy style. ''I'll tell you one thing, Mr. Kuroda. I wish to goodness you'd been around earlier in the week. Higashida's a very able young officer and I couldn't possibly have done without his help. But there were obvious limits to his authority and I was to say the least of it in a very ambiguous position as far as Takada was concerned.''

''You'll enjoy running your own division, sir. I'm already excited at the idea of running this one even for a week or two.''

''My guess is that it'll be more like a matter of months, and depending on how you handle it you could be in with a chance of promotion. I sat in for the commander at the last meeting of the Hyogo prefectural public safety committee and one of the main items on the agenda was the desperate shortage of experienced local officers at inspector level.''

''Is that why they're putting you in at Nada, sir? I was a bit puzzled when you told me because you're a National Police Agency man yourself, aren't you? I thought government officials like you only filled senior posts in prefectural headquarters.''

''That's broadly true, but exceptions are made here and there up and down the country. Ah, here we are already.'' The massive torii that formed the entrance to the grounds of the Inari Shrine loomed before them black against the slaty evening sky. ''I'd be interested to know how you plan to handle Horiuchi and his unsavory friends.''

Kuroda paused about twenty yards short of the entrance and stood without speaking for a moment. Two men wearing short *happi*-coats over ordinary trousers and with strips of cloth tied as sweatbands round their heads were fiddling with huge paper lanterns attached to the uprights of the torii, and as Otani and Kuroda watched first one and then the other was switched on. The lantern on the left, like the *happi*-coats the men were wearing, was emblazoned with the two Chinese characters meaning ''Inari''; the one on the right with two different ones meaning ''Shrine.'' People were already walking into the shrine and the sudden illumination brought the whole scene to bustling life.

''Very carefully,'' Kuroda said eventually. ''With all respect to you, sir, I'm not going to rush into anything before I've looked very carefully into your theory, and that's going to take time. Being pretty sure Horiuchi's up to no good is a far cry from being able to make out a solid case against him. And the fact that there'll certainly be a few thugs here tonight doesn't mean a thing. They're always around at any sizable open-air market and fair. As a rule they give no trouble. Quite the reverse, in fact. It's in their interest to make sure everything goes smoothly. I'm just going to keep my eyes open, frankly.''

''I quite agree. The tekiya have policed open-air markets for centuries. Great believers in law and order, they are, and the percentage they take from the stallholders is usually reasonable enough. That wasn't quite what I was getting at. In itself this monthly ennichi is perfectly harmless, I'm quite sure. And very likely Horiuchi won't even put in an appearance this evening. On the other hand I'm afraid that whatever you decide to do about him you're going to have to take some sort of action against his wife in the near future.''

Kuroda made no immediate reply, and Otani didn't press him as they strolled into the outer precinct, which had been transformed into a noisy cross between a marketplace and a fairground. It was still quite easy to move about even though there must already have been a couple of hundred people there and many more were now streaming in through the torii. Some were wandering about on their own, but there were many couples, mothers with children and what looked like complete families. Children were jumping up and down, squealing with excitement, most of them having already acquired balloons, cheap plastic toys or toffee apples. Otani noticed one wide-eyed little girl delicately nibbling at the edges of a ball of candy-floss bigger than her own head and experienced a pang of nostalgia: that was exactly the way Akiko had tackled candy-floss when she was very small.

Although it wasn't yet quite dark every stall was extravagantly lit and the cheery brightness all around made it seem that night had long since fallen. Most of the illuminations consisted of strings of plain and colored electric bulbs, but there were also plenty of old-fashioned kerosene pressure lamps hissing away as well as up-to-the-minute butane versions. The majority of the traders bawling affably at potential customers neither looked like crooks nor showed the slightest sign of being intimidated by gangsters. On the contrary, everyone seemed to be having a thoroughly good time. Otani and Kuroda passed rather quickly along a lane of stalls specializing in cheap household goods and children's clothes, and as they turned the corner Otani stopped and sniffed the air.

"Over that way," he said. "I fancy some fried noodles." In fact when they reached the line of foodstalls the variety of enticing sights and savory smells made it difficult for him to choose among small whole cuttlefish grilled with soy sauce, chicken kebabs and the noodles he had first thought of and now saw being vigorously tossed about and banged up and down in a huge wok by a beefy perspiring young woman with an enchanting smile. He temporized by buying a few sticks of the chicken kebabs to eat while he was making up his mind, and somewhat to his surprise saw that Kuroda had invested in a large, red and vulgar-looking ketchup-smeared sausage on a stick. He had thought him a more refined sort of man.

"I imagined you'd be eating at the inn later on," Kuroda said after they had each made inroads on their purchases. "I hope it's all right there, by the way."

"No, I told them I wouldn't want an evening meal tonight either. It's perfectly all right for a couple of nights, thanks. Slightly more rough and ready than the Tokiwa, but the people are pleasant and at least it doesn't seem to have a resident fox spirit. All the same I'll be glad to get back to my own home tomorrow."

"I'd like to ask you something, sir." Kuroda edged back so that he was partly in shadow and Otani joined him. "Following on what you said a while ago about Horiuchi's wife. You really are convinced she's in the clear so far as the actual killing's concerned?"

"Yes, I am. She's a clever woman and a very good actress, so it won't be easy for you to break her down. But you have the Polaroid photo of her with Craig Kington in her own house. Nothing exactly indecent about it, but highly compromising. She can't possibly deny being on affectionate terms with him. So I think she's sensible enough to do a deal if you make it clear that there's no particular need for her husband to know about the relationship. My guess is that she'll eventually admit that she was in the habit of slipping out of the house at night even when her husband was there to meet Kington—possibly on the pretext of walking the dog—and entertaining him in the house itself during Horiuchi's frequent absences. I'm as sure as I can be that Etsuko Suekawa found out about this, that she became furiously jealous, followed Kington that night and attacked him as soon as the couple parted. Finally, I think that as soon as

Naomi Horiuchi heard about the murder she rang Takada, the family friend, and begged him to keep her name out of it.''

"I see. And you think that one reason why she seemed so cool and collected about it all—apart from being a good actress—is that she might almost in a way have been relieved? That the affair with Kington was beginning to be too much for her to handle?"

"Something like that, perhaps."

"All right, but I still don't see how that pins the murder on Etsuko Suekawa. If you're right and Mrs. Horiuchi had gone back into the house there were no witnesses to the actual killing. Even Kington himself might have died not knowing who'd attacked him."

"Oh, come on, now! She was there in the room when Mrs. Kazama turned up and started exorcising the old woman. She realized the fox would sooner or later name her, slipped out of the room and got away while she had the chance. You heard that miserable specimen of a husband of hers say she'd taunted him to his face in the past by saying how good Kington was in bed. You're right, we may never find her, but if we ever do she'll confess, mark my words."

Kuroda coughed deprecatingly. "Well and good if she does, but there's still a big snag, sir."

"Oh? What snag is that?"

"Well, you see, the fox—good grief, you've got me calling it that now—the fox didn't actually name Etsuko Suekawa. Not even indirectly. You weren't there at the end, of course. But it just went on yelling and jeering and making a noise like a machine gun until suddenly Mrs. Kazama sort of stabbed in its direction with her fingers and it gave a kind of groan and then said, 'I'm pissed off with you lot. I'm going where I'll be appreciated.' Mori said it was those stabbing movements—a sword *mudra* he called them—that did the trick. Anyway, old Mrs. Suekawa seemed as right as rain after that. Pathetically grateful, in fact."

"Like a *machine gun*, did you say?"

"Yes, you know, like kids do when they're playing war games, ta-ka-ta-ka-ta-ka—"

140

"Oh, you stupid *idiot*! No no, not you, *me*!" Otani added hastily as he saw Kuroda draw himself up stiffly. "I've got it all hopelessly wrong! But in that case, where the hell *is* she?"

"I'm sorry, I don't quite—"

"Mr. Kuroda, you presumably have one or two plain-clothes men here this evening?"

"Two, apart from myself, yes—"

"Round them up, will you, and join me at the Horiuchi house. You know where it is? Up in the inner precinct up the path to the left of the main sanctuary building . . ." Without waiting for a reply Otani ducked between a popcorn vendor and a man selling goldfish in plastic bags and hurried toward the steps. A certain amount of light spilled on to them from the fairground area but Otani's eyes were still adjusted to the brilliance of the stalls and he stumbled, falling at the feet of the stone fox which had so unnerved him a few nights before. It held no terrors for him now, and he picked himself up, dusted himself down and made his way past the shrine office toward the path.

"Well, well, well. The interfering Otani yet again!" The voice came from the black pool of shadow behind the building and stopped Otani in his tracks, but he managed to answer in a calm enough voice.

"I'm glad I'm in time, Takada. If you're carrying a gun, drop it. My support team are on their way."

"Guns are noisy things. I prefer a knife, as you seem to have gathered. And I know every corner of this place. I shall deal with you and then if you do have support—which I very much doubt—I shall disappear before their eye—*aargh*—" A grunt of mingled pain and surprise prevented him from finishing the sentence.

"No you won't, Inspector. You're under arrest."

Otani sagged at the knees with relief at the sound of the firm young voice, the knife clattering to the gravel and the click of handcuffs. "Higashida! Thank heaven you turned up!"

"I nearly didn't." The voice was now stiff with offense. "I got the impression you had no further use for me now that Mr. Kuroda's back. But Noriko-chan insisted."

"I . . . I'm truly sorry, Higashida. I didn't mean it to seem like that. But how, how on earth—"

"Mori-sensei told us to keep an eye on the Horiuchi house and prevent the, er, prisoner entering. Noriko-chan and I have been here since this morning with a pair of binoculars. We saw you arrive and then spotted . . . the accused slipping into the compound after you. We've had him under observation ever since." Followed by Noriko, Higashida dragged Takada out of the shadows and Otani looked at the prisoner in disgust.

"And to think I was soft enough to give you a chance! Good evening, and thank you very much indeed, Miss Ito." As he spoke Kuroda came pounding up, two more men on his heels. Otani turned to him. "The fox did name the murderer after all. It wasn't imitating a machine gun, it was saying, 'Takadatakadatakada.' Over and over again. As Mori-sensei realized."

Chapter 19

"**A**ND SO,**" TADAO MORI CONCLUDED WITH SOME-
thing of a flourish, "in the circumstances I have decided to
foreclose the mortgage and take possession of the Tokiwa
myself."

"You're going to run an inn?"

Mori looked at Otani haughtily. "I infer from the incre-
dulity of your tone, sir, that you question my ability to suc-
ceed in such an enterprise. Do you not credit me with an
intelligence superior to that of the contemptible Suekawa who
has for a good many years contrived to manage the inn?"

Kuroda made no attempt to conceal his smile. "But you've
just been telling us what a mess he made of it," he pointed
out. "How he got deeper and deeper in debt to you year by
year until the whole place was mortgaged up to the hilt.
Anyway, you've made it very clear that it's your property to
do what you like with and it's none of our business. What
does interest me is the news that Suekawa plans to clear out
of Sumoto. Leave Awaji altogether, in fact." He looked at
Otani. "Do you see any objection to that, Inspector?"

"Well, you might want to hold him for a few days and
check to see whether he's involved in any way with Hori-

uchi's enterprises, but I think we have to accept that he isn't implicated in the murder. And when he does leave town it would be wise to keep tabs on him. He could very well lead you to his wife.''

"That will not happen," Mori said confidently.

"You seem very sure of that."

"I am. There will be a divorce."

Otani stared at him. "I'm aware that you and your own late wife arranged the Suekawa marriage many years ago. Mrs. Suekawa mentioned it to me herself. No doubt you've observed the course of their relationship since."

"Of course. That is one of the continuing duties of a go-between. In any case, Etsuko Suekawa is a distant cousin of mine by marriage and has always confided in me. She has been contemplating divorce for some time and the events of this week have made it inevitable."

Kuroda intervened again. The three men were in Takada's old office, Kuroda having slipped without hesitation into Takada's chair and left Otani in no doubt that he regarded himself as being in charge of the proceedings. "Be that as it may, sir, Mrs. Suekawa has disappeared in highly suspicious circumstances. Her future marital status is of much less interest to me than the fact that she is wanted for questioning. In view of what you've just told us it occurs to me that she may at some stage get in touch with you. If she does I would urge you to advise her to come forward."

"Why? Do you propose to charge her with some offense? Of complicity with Takada perhaps? Pray remember that I am an attorney at law. In that capacity I fail to see that now that you have caught your murderer and he has confessed, Mrs. Suekawa has any duty to submit herself to you for questioning."

Otani sat up straight. "May I, Mr. Kuroda? Thank you. Mr. Mori, I am well aware that had it not been for your highly irregular interference in police business Takada might have killed or seriously injured me yesterday evening. I am grateful indeed, and it would be both ungracious and absurd for me to attempt to hector you now. But Mrs. Suekawa

144

really does have a great many questions to answer, and so do you.''

"I cannot speak for Mrs. Suekawa, but you and your colleague are welcome to apply to me for enlightenment.''

Kuroda smiled and opened his hands in a gesture of appeal. "Please go ahead if you would, Inspector Otani. I've been involved in this case for less than forty-eight hours, and need all the enlightenment I can get.''

"Thank you. Mr. Mori, I was not myself present during the closing stages of the exorcism. So I didn't hear the fox repeatedly gabble the name Takada in such a way that Mr. Kuroda here got the impression that it was childishly imitating a machine gun. Not an unreasonable inference given the way it had been behaving earlier. You, on the other hand, obviously did recognize the name.''

"I did, yes, and all became crystal clear to me at that moment. I realized why and how the fox had used Takada to accomplish the killing. Takada was a frequent visitor to the Horiuchi house, so the guard dog knew and accepted him. He was besotted with Mrs. Horiuchi, though I can hardly believe that she could possibly have encouraged such a fatuous admirer. He also detested the very idea of the presence in Sumoto of the two foreigners.''

"The first time you mentioned his name to me you called him a buffoon, the second time a poltroon. Now he's fatuous. Hardly terms I should myself apply to a murderer.''

Mori looked from one to the other of the two police officers over his glasses. "The wretched Takada deserves each of those epithets and more. His essential weakness of character made him an ideal vehicle for the fox.''

"You really do believe in the fox, don't you?'' Kuroda was gazing at Mori in open wonderment.

"I most certainly do, young man, and in view of your presence in that room when Mrs. Kazama by the power of the Lord Fudo finally succeeded in banishing it to Izumo I am astounded that you appear to remain skeptical. I can assure you that I should certainly not have begun to contemplate assuming the ownership of the Tokiwa if the fox-spirit remained in residence.''

Otani tried again. "I'm sorry, sensei, but I still haven't understood what the fox had against Craig Kington."

"For an intelligent man you can be remarkably obtuse at times, Inspector. The American was a ladies' man, as you well know. Being most of the time on watch through the eyes of old Mrs. Suekawa, the fox knew that Kington had visited the Tokiwa and begun the process of charming Etsuko, a frustrated, passionate woman. Possibly the fox accompanied Etsuko when she visited the young man for so-called private lessons. The important point is that the fox was aware that the Tokiwa household was in a precarious position in any case, and feared that Etsuko might completely lose her head over Kington, run away with him perhaps. Perverse though it undoubtedly was, the fox had a sense of responsibility toward its host family. So it decided that Kington had to be eliminated. Now needless to say the fox spent a good deal of time prowling about the Inari Shrine by night; and it had often seen Kington near the Horiuchi house, and Takada shadowing him. The rest is surely obvious."

"Not quite," Otani said. "When I myself realized that what Mr. Kuroda here had heard was in fact the name Takada I saw much as you did that he could indeed have killed the American and indeed almost certainly had. It then struck me that having had time to brood over his predicament he might well attempt to kill the priest Horiuchi. Horiuchi was not only in a sense responsible for his downfall; he was the one person who could produce evidence of the true extent of Takada's corruption. That, of course, was why he had been so anxious to prevent my interrogating Horiuchi properly. And I guessed he would lose no time in making the attempt, would probably move as soon as the effects of the sedative his doctor had given him had worn off. Now what I'd very much like to know is why *you* thought Horiuchi might be in danger from Takada, especially as the fox had been bested once and for all and sent howling back to Izumo. You're not claiming it deceived even Mrs. Kazama and simply transferred itself to Takada's family, are you?"

Mori smiled serenely. "Not at all. The fox will trouble nobody in Sumoto again, you may be sure of that. My reasoning was much less complicated. Having made a study of these phenomena, I knew that once bereft of the influence of the fox Takada would become unhinged. My dear fellow, I'm well aware that you think I'm probably off my head myself, but that is your problem, not mine. I think that if you were to inquire of people in a position to give an informed opinion you would find that my reputation in Sumoto is rather different.'' He paused and flicked a speck of dust from his lapel.

"That in fact I am known as a good lawyer and a reasonably astute financier. I keep a close eye on what goes on in this town, gentlemen. I know all about Horiuchi's various enterprises and his links with organized crime, and I know all about Takada's greed and folly. I, too, thought that he would try to silence Horiuchi, and that is why I suggested to the police officer who is Noriko Ito's friend that he should watch over the Horiuchi house. I saw no reason why that amiable young man should not be in a position to emerge with personal credit from this affair. You and I arrived at the same conclusion and by the same route, Inspector.''

"Well, I don't know about you, but it *is* Saturday morning and after a weird conversation like that I fancy a beer,'' Kuroda said, lingering at the entrance to the building after they had ushered Mori out and watched him jauntily turn the corner out of sight. "We've got time before we need to leave for Iwaya.''

"All right. I'd enjoy some sushi with it, though. That place over there seems to be opening up.''

A few minutes later they were perched companionably beside each other on stools at the slab of smooth white wood which formed the counter of the *sushiya*, sharing a bottle of Kirin beer and watching the master construct the first two pairs of sushi for them. "Old Mori has reminded me to mention Higashida again before I go,'' Otani said. "He has performed quite outstandingly, you know. I'm only sorry that in all the confusion last night I didn't really say goodbye to him properly. Give him my thanks and best wishes, would you? I'll write him a note when I get back. And with your agreement I'm going to recommend him for an official commendation.''

"Very nice of you. It can't have been easy for him to put the cuffs on a senior inspector, even if he had announced his intention of knifing you. Higashida's a bit young to be made up to senior patrolman, but I suppose he could be encouraged to take the exams and try for the fast stream.'' Kuroda picked up one of the shrimp sushi in front of him, dipped it in soy sauce and deftly popped it into his mouth.

Otani had already disposed of a pair topped with oblong pieces of omelette, teased his taste-buds with some pickled ginger and moved on to tuna. "Look, there's really no need for you to go all the way to Iwaya with me, you know,'' he said. "I'm grateful as it is for the use of your car, and I'm sure Mori's given you quite enough to keep you busy here.''

Kuroda chuckled. "He has indeed. Well, I feel I ought to do the honors, but if you're really sure . . .''

"I am. As you say, it *is* Saturday.'' He sighed briefly. "This business of the vanishing Mrs. Suekawa's going to nag at me, confound it. You will give me a ring if you find out where she went, won't you?''

"Of course.''

"I'm glad Mrs. Kazama got rid of that damned fox.''

"Oh, come on, you know as well as I do that old woman was just suffering from delusions. Mrs. Kazama's therapy certainly worked on her, but all this fox talk is just eyewash.''

Otani looked steadily at the younger man. He had noticed earlier that Kuroda had stopped calling him "sir,'' and now his manner was becoming distinctly overfamiliar. "You're in charge here for the time being, Mr. Kuroda, and it's not for me to tell you how to do your job. But since I'm on the point of leaving I'll take the liberty of counseling you against overconfidence. I went up a number of blind alleys myself this week, and I'd remind you that it took the combined and very remarkable talents of Mrs. Kazama and Mr. Mori to tease out the essential truth of the matter. I accept that I've been using what must strike you as being a very fanciful vocabulary, but then I've had some personal encounters with what I intend to go on thinking of as the Suekawa fox. You'd

148

be wise to cultivate Mori and treat his opinions with respect. And now I really ought to be on my way, I think. No, this is my treat, I insist.'' He swung off his stool and went to the end of the counter where the cash-box was, taking out his wallet as he did so and giving Kuroda time to swallow the reproof.

By the time they had crossed the road to where the police car was already parked outside the headquarters building the brief moment of constraint between them was forgotten, and Otani smiled at Kuroda with unforced warmth as he took his leave, assuring him yet again that he wouldn't dream of allowing him to go all the way to Iwaya only to turn round and drive straight back again.

Kuroda was holding the car door open and checking with the driver that Otani's belongings were on board when Otani heard once more from behind him what had become a familiar voice. ''Inspector! Gentlemen! A moment, please!'' He turned, and gaped.

Silver-topped stick raised on high as though he were leading a group of tourists, Tadao Mori was as spry as ever. At his side, Etsuko Suekawa looked radiant. Her face glowed with happiness, she was beautifully turned out, and she looked about thirty. Otani found it very hard to credit that less than forty-eight hours earlier this woman had been a crumpled, haggard, defeated-looking heap. Kuroda too was goggling at the pair of them.

''As soon as I returned to my house, where Mrs. Suekawa has been my guest, I conveyed to her the gist of our recent conversation,'' Mori said calmly. ''Mrs. Suekawa was anxious that you should not misinterpret her desire for a few days of privacy as anything more than that, and indeed wished if possible to bid farewell to the inspector.''

His words reached Otani as though through several layers of gauze, while the beautiful eyes held his own for a long, eloquent moment and the full lips trembled almost imperceptibly. He went on staring at her in helpless admiration when she spoke.

''I'm so glad we were in time to catch you, Inspector. I'm afraid your stay at the Tokiwa was hardly restful, but . . . it has been an honor to make your acquaintance, and I do hope we shall meet again one day. I wanted you to know that as soon as my divorce has been arranged—"

"The dear lady has consented to become my wife!" Mori crowed.

Chapter 20

WHEN THE POLICE DRIVER PULLED UP WITH A FLOURISH at the Iwaya ferry terminal, got out and opened the passenger door for him with a smart salute, Otani came to with a start and clambered out of the car in some confusion. He had no recollection whatever of the details of the drive from Sumoto, of passing for the fourth time that week through the villages Takada had so laboriously pointed out to him on the first day and which he had seen again from the taxi he had shared with Higashida on the way to intercept Horiuchi and then once more through the window of the trundling bus.

Somehow he managed to collect himself enough to take charge of his bundle of belongings and thank the driver, who had to be dissuaded from waiting until the ferry left. Once the car had disappeared from sight, Otani ambled away from the little booking office and wandered aimlessly along the waterfront, slipping back into a state somewhere between reverie and trance.

The image of Etsuko Suekawa's face rose up again in his consciousness as it had absorbed him during the journey. It was the tranquillity of her expression which made her seem so youthful: as though the exorcism of her mother-in-law had somehow cleansed, softened and calmed her too. In retrospect it seemed to Otani that the aura of sensuality which had emanated from her when he first met her had been almost frighteningly powerful and indeed out of her own control; as though he would have needed only to reach out and touch her to set off a fierce, hungry and utterly uninhibited whirlwind of sexual desire.

Now, by contrast, it was as if her sexuality were no longer autonomous, driving her perhaps against her will. The new Etsuko was confident, serene, in charge of herself, still well aware of her resplendent femininity but no longer—well, confound it, there *was* no other appropriate word, no longer *possessed*. And when she had looked at him during that long, lingering moment it had been without embarrassment. No, but rather with a sort of friendly, tender complicity, as though they had come safely through a bruising experience together; one that neither of them could or should forget.

As he stood there looking out at the quiet harbor with its clutter of small fishing boats, the sharp smells of sea and tar in his nostrils, Otani experienced a growing sense of elation. He recognized it. It was akin to the feeling he still remembered from his schooldays when vacation time came round, and to some extent recaptured every time he was transferred from one police appointment to a new assignment. He was now free to start thinking about taking command of the Nada division. It was a challenge he was on the whole quite looking forward to measuring himself against, and it was good to have a full week to clear both his desk at headquarters and his mind in preparation.

Meantime he was properly alone for the first time in nearly a week, and well and truly off duty. In a couple of hours or so he would be at home in Rokko. At least he had advance warning of the problems that his daughter Akiko's revolutionary enthusiasm might give rise to, but compared with a vicious fox-spirit a mere Maoist ought to be simplicity itself to handle with patience and love.

His mood abruptly changed when he thought of Hanae. Patient, gentle, good-humored Hanae who had sounded so happy to hear from him when he rang late the previous evening to tell her that he was coming home. He realized that he must still have been high on adrenalin in the aftermath of the brief but violent flurry of activity at the shrine which culminated in Takada's arrest, and that Hanae might well have thought he had been drinking.

For he had said nothing to her about the threat to himself; merely that the investigation had been more or less satisfactorily concluded and that the local man could tidy up any remaining odds and ends. He was never very communicative about his work, and Hanae wouldn't expect more than a laconic, vague account of what he had been doing. All the same, having consulted her about magical foxes he owed her an explanation of his curiosity on the subject.

What more did he owe her? What *had* actually happened between Etsuko and himself? The episode in the bath had been real enough. His flesh still tingled whenever he remembered it, and he rather thought he would remember it quite often in the future. But later? When he had blundered drunkenly back to the Tokiwa after his eerie experience at the shrine? He had a vague recollection of being welcomed by Etsuko, tolerant and friendly. He thought he could even remember an appealing fragrance about her as she stood there in her yukata. But after that? Had she helped him upstairs or had he managed to get up them by himself, hauling himself on his hands and knees like a drunk in a cartoon? Had it all been a dream, that yearning, frenzied struggling and coupling? The sweating and straining that preceded his sudden return to bleak, despairing consciousness, alone in a tangle of bedding, his head throbbing, his mouth dry, his breath foul? Or had he—both of them—been seduced? He knew only that he had hated himself during the dark hours that followed, the hours when for some reason he—among the least poetic of men—had sat there scribbling haiku one after another, crumpling each sheet and tossing it from him as soon as it was done.

"Don't look so sad. There's another one in half an hour."

Otani whirled round, blinking in confusion as he first focused on the face of Noriko Ito and then registered the presence of Higashida standing behind her, grinning from ear to ear. "I . . . I'm so sorry. I was miles away. Oh, I see. Yes, I do seem to have missed the ferry, don't I. How nice to see you both . . . but what brings you here?"

"We came to see you off, of course. We saw you arrive and were going to come and speak to you right away but you looked as though you wanted to be alone, so we left you to it for a while."

"But I told Noriko-chan you wouldn't want to miss the next ferry too, and we finally took a chance."

Otani smiled at them both, fully conscious and back in the world of everyday life at last. "So it's 'Noriko-chan' to her face now, is it?"

"Oh, I've made it very clear to him that he'd better not try taking me for granted."

"Well, I was telling Mr. Koruda just an hour ago that Patrolman Higashida seems to possess what Mr. Mori would probably call a modicum of intelligence, so I expect he'll bear your warning in mind. Thank you, both of you. For coming here to see me off, and for everything you've both done this week. Have you heard that the Suekawas are getting a divorce and that Mrs. Suekawa and Mr. Mori are planning to get married afterward?"

Noriko pulled a comical face. "Yes. I heard. He was so excited he rang me up and told me first thing. Me, of all people! It was all I could do to stop myself laughing out loud." She turned to Higashida and pushed him away with mock severity. "Off you go for a minute. I've got something private to discuss with the inspector." Looking slightly bemused but still exuding good humor, Higashida wandered out of earshot and Noriko grabbed Otani by the arm.

"I've been thinking about those haiku of yours. Two of them really are quite good, you know." She gazed out to sea and recited in a sonorous voice quite different from her normal speech:

> " 'My heart yearns, confused.
> I reached out, hot with passion,
> Into emptiness.' "

"Really, Miss Ito, you embarrass me. I think the kindest thing you could do for me would be to forget all about that dreadful doggerel I was foolish enough to leave lying about."

"They weren't all doggerel by any means, you're much too modest. I'm not quite sure about 'hot with passion.' That is a bit of a cliché, quite honestly. What about 'dazed with passion' instead? Or 'bewitched with lust'? Same number of syllables. I'm sorry I said that about Etsuko to you, by the way. I could tell you hated it. Promise not to laugh at me, but I was a bit jealous, actually."

"I won't laugh at you, no. In fact I feel honored. Apart from wishing the ground would open up and swallow me, that is. And now I'm going to buy my ticket. Look, the next ferry's already coming in."

Noriko's hand was still on his arm. "I haven't finished with you yet. You wrote a much better one:

" 'Beckoned by fox fire
I lost my way, but then you
Called me safely home.'

"That was the one that made me cry. Do write it out properly when you get back, with a brush." She released his arm and reached into the holdall she was carrying. "This is one I wrote for you," she said, awkwardly pushing a large envelope into Otani's hand. Slowly he opened the flap and drew out a square of thick card, its surface protected by a flap of translucent rice-paper.

"Justice is a dream.
Warmer far, humanity
In a kindly man."

"I'm afraid my calligraphy isn't a patch on Mr. Mori's."
Otani looked at her, none too sure that he could speak.

"It's beautiful. And I shall treasure it. I thank you from the bottom of my heart, Noriko-chan."

Postlude:
The Present

"**Y**OU AREN'T REALLY CROSS WITH YOUR GRANDFA-
ther, are you?"

"But I wanted to go Iwaya to meet you," Kazuo Shimizu
said, clinging to the remains of his sense of grievance.

"Well, we couldn't have done," his mother said briskly.
"In the first place we didn't know exactly what time they
were coming, in the second place the bus stops just on the
other side of the road, and in the third place you were at
school anyway."

"Tell you what," Otani said. "If your mother and father
say yes, on Saturday or Sunday perhaps we'll go off on the
bus on our own and see the whirlpools at Naruto. How about
that?"

"Just you and me?"

"Just you and me."

"All right. Do you want to come and see my things now?"

Left to themselves, Hanae and her daughter looked at each
other. "I'm sorry Akira wasn't there to welcome you,
Mother. The very first time you come to stay, too. But he
had to go to Sumoto to register the purchase agreement for
an extra piece of land. He said he'd be back by five at the
latest."

Hanae looked round the bright, simply furnished but spacious kitchen. When she had first seen the old house they had bought along with the smallholding she had thought it dreadfully insanitary-looking and inconvenient, but she had to admit they had done wonders with it. It was now a solid, justly proportioned, peaceful and welcoming home, utterly different from the poky, tasteless, expensive "executive-type" house in Senri New Town she had once nevertheless thought them insane to leave.

"Goodness, are you thinking of expanding already?"

Akiko smiled, pride and good-humored exasperation vying for supremacy in her expression. "You know Akira. I honestly think that if he found himself shipwrecked on a desert island within six months he'd have formed a development corporation. The tomatoes and cucumbers have been a great success already, but he reckons the trend is toward more exotic fruit and vegetables. And one of our neighbors wanted to sell up and go and live in one of these new retirement resorts in Australia that are all the rage. It's only about half a hectare but even so when we've got the hydroponics equipment installed and working it'll make us one of the biggest enterprises in this district."

Hanae nodded, though she had only a sketchy idea of what her daughter was talking about. "Well, I'm sure you'll do well. The life certainly seems to suit you, dear." Akiko did indeed look both relaxed and fit, loafing there with casual elegance in jeans and a checked shirt cut like a man's. "I expect you've made a lot of new friends?"

"A few. I do my bit for the PTA at Kazuo's school and meet other mums there but I try not to get too involved. We see a good deal of one couple about our own age that we like a lot. He's our lawyer in Sumoto, actually. Akira's with him this afternoon. He and his wife have helped us in all sorts of other ways, and become personal friends. I think it's quite possible that sooner or later we may go into some sort of business partnership with them. I expect you'll meet them while you're here, they often drop in over the weekend."

* * *

Otani hesitated before walking under the torii at the main entrance to the Inari Shrine, but then took a few paces forward and looked around the outer precinct. The kindergarten was still there and so was the parking lot, but the breezy, somewhat intimidating slogans and banners seemed to have gone, and the paintwork had a weathered, slightly shabby look about it. It wasn't that the shrine seemed to be exactly neglected. There were plenty of people about, including a group of high-school girls in uniform posing for a commemorative photograph against the background of the stone steps up to the inner precinct, in front of the smaller torii and the stone foxes he remembered so well. No, it was just that the Inari Shrine had lost the slick gloss that had characterized it twenty years earlier, and Otani thought it much improved as a result.

He walked up the steps, noticing that one of the guardian foxes had lost an ear and that patches of yellow lichen had become established here and there on both of them. The shrine office was open, and Otani paid fifty yen for a fortune to a pretty girl in the red and white robes of a shrine maiden, her glossy black hair enclosed at the back in a hollow, gilded tube. She watched him pick up and shake the long hexagonal container on the counter and ease one of the bamboo rods inside through the small hole at the top.

"Number nineteen, please," he said after peering at its flattened end, and the girl handed him a printed slip of paper she took from the appropriate little pigeonhole in the bank of them at her side. Otani studied it. Middling Good Fortune, it said. Nothing like as good as Great Good Fortune but an improvement on just plain Good Fortune, the worst possible one to select. Good Fortune in fact usually portended bankruptcy, ill-health and other disasters, but of course the prophecy could easily be rendered null and void by folding the paper in a strip and tying it to a tree or some other suitable object near the inner sanctuary.

Middling good fortune. Reasonable enough at his age, Otani thought. He studied the spidery phonetic script of the details. Health, not too bad. Money, no serious problems provided he avoided extravagance. Take care on the roads. Cultivate friends . . . cultivate friends.

"Gomen kudasai!" There was no immediate reply. Otani was already regretting his impulsiveness and turned to leave again with a certain sense of relief. It was enough to know that the Tokiwa Inn was still there, still in business and, he had been assured, prospering. He was a silly, sentimental old fool to—

"Hai, irasshaimase! So sorry to have kept you waiting. Please step up. Such a lovely day, isn't—*Ara!* Is it . . . can it be . . . is it really you?"

"Mrs. Mori, I think? Good afternoon. Yes. I'm Otani. It's been a long time."

" . . . so as I say, I should never have dreamed of intruding had it not been for this extraordinary coincidence of my daughter and her husband being good friends of the Higashidas. I was staggered when they walked in. And so were they, I think."

"No, I don't think they were, you know. Noriko told me soon after they got to know the Shimizus that she'd discovered that Mrs. Shimizu is your daughter, but for some reason she didn't want you to find out. She's made it her business to keep track of you all these years."

"I wish I'd known."

Etsuko Mori shrugged elegantly. She had lost weight, but looked trim and fashionable in a Western-style silk dress. An extension had been built on to the inn, and they were sitting in armchairs in a smart bar which had been fitted in roughly where Otani remembered the kitchen as having been. "It was probably for the best."

"I blame myself for not looking through the personnel lists from time to time and realizing that he'd left the force and become a lawyer. Taken over your late husband's practice in fact? Please accept my condolences, by the way."

"Thank you. It was a great loss, but we had ten very happy years together and he was ready to go when the time came. I expect he seemed a very dry old stick to you, but he could be such *fun*, you know. Very few people realized that, but I knew him when he was young. That's when I first fell in love

159

with him, of course. My only regret is that he didn't ask me to marry him as soon as his first wife died, but by then the poor man was tormented by guilt.''

"Guilt?''

Etsuko smiled. She looked her age now, Otani thought, but her lips were still soft and full, and she could still hold his eyes with hers. "Yes. He'd had to arrange my marriage in a bit of a hurry but he thought it a sensible enough one. It wasn't until later that my former husband started running this place. Then old Mrs. Suekawa started going on about the fox, and my husband, my late husband Tadao that is, became obsessed with the subject. He was convinced that he had been instrumental in bringing a curse on me too, and tried to make up for it by saving all he could and investing it in my name—also of course in effect subsidizing the Tokiwa all those years.''

"I wonder why he didn't try to get Mrs. Kazama to exorcise the old lady much sooner?''

"I don't think it occurred to him that it could be done until Noriko suggested it shortly before the murder. The Itos lived near Mrs. Kazama and Noriko had known her most of her life, but obviously Noriko didn't find out about the fox-spirit until she came to work at the Tokiwa.''

"All sorts of questions have stayed with me these past twenty years, you know.''

"Me too, Superintendent. It is superintendent now, isn't it?'' Her smile was composed, slightly quizzical, and Otani looked away in confusion.

"Er, yes. Not that it's of any importance. About Noriko, though. Could you satisfy my curiosity about two things I've never been able to work out?''

"I'll try. What two things?''

"Well, the biggest mystery to me is how on earth a girl like that came to take a job as a maid in an inn in the first place. The other is a silly thing that still bothers me from time to time. It's this: on the morning I left Sumoto, the morning Mori-sensei brought you to police headquarters and announced your engagement, he had already telephoned Noriko to tell her. Now why would he do that?''

160

"Why, there's no mystery! He *was* her father, after all."

"*What?*"

Etsuko Mori was obviously enjoying herself. "Yes, and I'm her mother. I told you I fell in love with him years ago. Oh no, he didn't take advantage of me; the reverse if anything. I stayed with the Itos for the birth and they fostered her for us. Noriko was told the truth when she was sixteen and quite soon became fond of her real father. Though of course she always thought of the Itos as her proper parents, and still does."

Otani nodded to himself as she went on, a dreamy expression on her face. "I'm afraid it took me a very long time to begin to break through her hostility to me. Noriko came to the Tokiwa because Tadao begged her to. He was so impressed by her communist convictions that he thought if anyone would be immune to the fox it would be her, and that she might somehow be able to get rid of it. But it began to bother even Noriko and she soon stopped living in. After a while she did begin to realize what I was going through with Suekawa and my mother-in-law, and her sympathy helped me more than she could ever have imagined."

"I'm deeply grateful to you for telling me," Otani said. "I liked Noriko from the first. Now I realize just how impressive she is." He sighed. "And to think I nearly didn't come here today! To tell you the truth, I was nervous about seeing you again, even long after the fox-spirit went away." He stood up but continued to look down at her, and Etsuko gazed up at him, still with that hint of secret satisfaction in her face.

"It wasn't an altogether horrible week for you, was it?" she said. "And even though it wasn't the happiest time of my life, I very much enjoyed getting to know *you* so well. You'll be a most welcome guest if you'd ever like to come back here for a few days, Superintendent." Then she stood up too.

"I'm only sorry we don't have a mixed bath any longer. They're against the municipal by-laws."

About the Author

JAMES MELVILLE was born in London in 1931. After studying philosophy, he was conscripted into the RAF. He later took up schoolteaching and adult education, and has spent many years overseas in cultural diplomacy and educational development. It was during several overseas assignments that he came to know, love, and write about Japan and the Japanese. He has two sons and is married to a textile artist. He continues to write novels in the Superintendent Otani series from his home in Herefordshire, England.